MW01234182

A BOOK BY C. M. MCLAIN

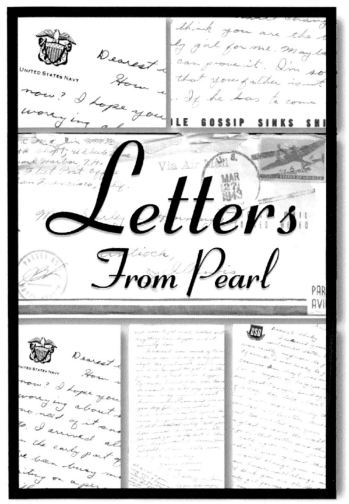

A LOVE STORY FROM WWII

Letters
From Pearl

A Novel By

C. M. McLain

Contact the Author:

Website: https://mclaincm.com

Email: lettersfrompearl@gmail.com

Instagram: @lettersfrompearl

Facebook: Letters From Pearl

Dedication

The book is dedicated to the memory of Clyde C. McLain and Shirley A. Hennings McLain's and the family they loved and nurtured following World War II.

Acknowledgments

Thanks to all my friends and family for their support and encouragement in this project. Especially Carole, my wonderful wife, travel partner and life-long friend, for her help, patience and encouragement in writing this book.

A special thank you to my long-time friend and Godmother, Betty Hanké Fischer, for all her help with the details of this book and for writing with me over the years. I am so thankful for her friendship with "Shirsh," my mother. Over the years, Betty and Shirley talked regularly by phone. "Bets" and "Shirsh" or "Shirl" for short, spoke with each other for the last time during Shirley's last days on earth, truly a friendship of life-long childhood companions. As a young boy, I remember how I loved playing throughout her house and how kind she was. I know why my mom liked her so much because I sure did. She was my "Aunt Betty" and my Godmother.

Style Notes: Quotations from Letters are in *Italic*. Text Notes or Comments are numbered at the bottom of the page in <u>10-point font.</u>

Terminology Notes: The US Navy uses different terms for vessels. A surface vessel is always referred to as a SHIP, and A submarine is always referred to as a BOAT. All vessels have been historically referred to by the pronouns SHE or HER. Military Time is always 24 hours, Midnight is 2400 hours, and Noon is 1200 hours. 0600 hours is 6 AM in the morning, 1800 hours is 6 PM in the evening.

Introduction

They have been called the "Greatest Generation." They were raised in poverty during the Great Depression of the 1930s. They were called upon to sacrifice everything for their country. Out of love, duty, and honor, they volunteered to serve and sacrifice to preserve the freedoms that we enjoy today and that are at great risk of being taken away once again by tyrannical elements. They gave all. Food, clothing, gasoline, metals, factories, labor, time, and more were given up for the war effort to stand behind and support those fighting for our liberties.

In the midst of that great World War, where men and women, combatants and civilians alike, died to preserve a way of life for the next generation, a love story grew in the shadows of the daily headlines of loss and victory. It has been more than eighty years since Clyde, my father, wrote to a young woman he met on Christmas Day 1942. I have finally opened the ribbon-tied bundles of letters and read the words hidden for all those years: letters of love and hope, a life lived in war. It is like seeing the world through my father's eyes and hearing his words of hope for their future together as if he were speaking through the years beside me. Over 600 letters were written from the end of 1942 to the end of 1945. The letters have been preserved in a steel, watertight sea chest that once held surplus U.S. Navy Radar parts since 1945. This chest most likely contained all the machinist tools that he had used in the Submarine Machine Shop at Pearl Harbor. They would have been shipped to him on the mainland after the war. Strangely enough, the letters from Shirley to Clyde never made it home from Pearl Harbor with the rest of his belongings. So, one can only speculate how she responded to his letters and what her side of the conversation must have been.

As a child, I would climb on the chest, sit on it, and make a fort out of it, but I was never allowed to open it or touch the letters Dad had written to Mom. Our family dragged that steel chest from house to house, across the Pacific, back to Hawaii, California, and finally to Idaho. Now that they have both passed from this life to the next, we have lost that connection to their younger lives and romance, except for these letters from Pearl Harbor, Hawaii, during World War II.

Letters from Pearl is my way of expressing my love, my grief, and my gratitude for their lives. They were truly part of the Greatest Generation. I hope you will enjoy reading history directly from my father's pen. Thanks.

Contents

One - The Returning

24 July, 1945. Tuesday, Clyde began boarding the Military Sea Transport Service (MSTS) ship in Pearl Harbor with his seabag over his shoulder and dressed in his spotless white uniform. He saluted the American flag at the stern of the ship, then turned to the Officer of the Deck and said, "Permission to come aboard, sir?" The O.D. returned the salute and said, "Permission Granted. Sign in and see the Deck Steward on the third deck below."

Clyde headed down to his bunk below deck. Stowed his gear and then went topside. About a half hour later, the loudspeaker announced, "Prepare to cast off all lines. Remove the gangway." Then, "Cast off stern lines." "Cast off bowlines." Then, the ship's airhorn blasted a long blast. The ship started to move away from the pier with the help of two tugboats. When the ship was safely away from the dock and headed to the main channel of Pearl Harbor Naval Base, the tugboats pulled away as the great MSTS ship headed toward the open Pacific Ocean. A few minutes later, the loudspeaker announced, "Man the rails," "Attention on deck," and "Salute," as the ship slowly passed the destroyed hulk of the USS Arizona battleship, where over 1800 men had been entombed since the Japanese invasion of 7 December 1941. Three and a half years had passed since then, but now all-hands-on-deck stand at attention, saluting until they have passed the

USS Arizona tomb. Leaving Pearl Harbor behind and only open seas lay ahead to the mainland USA.

A sailor standing at the rails next to Clyde said, "Where you headed?" Clyde replied, "Back State-side. This is my first leave in thirty-two months. I hope to make Chicago before I have to return to Pearl."

"Good luck. I've gotta make Kansas City, where I have a gal waiting for me." The two sailors walked back to the hatch leading to the lower decks. Clyde smiled, "Yeah, me too. I haven't seen her since January '43. I hope she still wants to see me. I've been writing to her every day."

"You take care; I gotta shove off now. Good luck to you. See ya around." The sailor descended below deck. Clyde headed down to his bunk for a rest before chow-call.

In his bunk room, Clyde was changing out of his Whites into his dungarees that feel more relaxed for the ocean journey. In the room, several guys were playing cards; there was a light air of relief to be on the way home and a break from the Pacific War.

The shipboard routine was typical: reveille at 0500 hours, shower and dress, report for roll call at 0600, and chow 0630. Clyde had not been on board since he left San Francisco Bay in February 1943. The morning routine on base in Pearl Harbor Submarine Machine Shop #2 was almost the same. Still, it was frequently altered by urgent repairs and upgrades required by the large fleet of submarines operating in the Pacific Theater.

Clyde grabbed his chow tray and looked for an open seat. "Mind if I join you, boys?" He sat down. "Thanks. How'd you guys get a ticket on this fancy cruise ship?" They laughed.

14

One sailor replied, "Been transferred to a new ship coming out of Frisco Bay." Another said, "They patched me up after our sub was hit on patrol. Going back for some special surgery to try and make my arm work again."

"Tuff break. Subs, huh?" said Clyde. "I have been working at the Sub Base Machine Shop since February '43. Been fixin' those damned Mark 14 torpedoes since I got there. We installed most of the radar units on the sub-fleet. And patched up several boats. One had an unexploded shell in her outer hull. The Skipper wanted to save it for a souvenir. So, when it was safe to work, I cut the casing up and made a cigarette ashtray for the Skipper." Clyde paused to take a bite. "I see this chow ain't any better than the Mess Hall in Pearl." They continued to talk. Each excused themselves from the table as they headed back to their sleeping compartments.

30 July, 1945. Six days had passed since Clyde left Pearl. A few days were marked with seasickness, and others lacked anything to do. Tired and weary from seasickness, Clyde was awakened from a sound sleep by the shipboard public address system announcement, "Uniform of the Day is Dress Blues. Prepare to Man the Rails as the ship passes under the Golden Gate Bridge in 30 minutes. All-hands-on deck to salute as we enter the Bay Area." A loud cheer could be heard throughout the ship. The crew knew that they had made it state-side without any wartime conflict. The fighting was over for them, at least for thirty days.

There is nothing much more beautiful than the Golden Gate Bridge with the orange dawn of sunrise behind it. A breathtaking, beautiful view punctuated with puffy fog clouds lingering in darker recesses of the bay waters. As the

MSTS ship slipped under the bridge, the captain blew a long blast on the ship's whistle to signal that they had arrived in the continental United States. The Main Deck was filled with sailors dressed in their best uniforms, standing at the rails, cheering and waving to anyone or anything in their path.

The ship's engines slowed as they passed Fort Mason, the Alcatraz Federal Prison known as the Rock, heading northeast past Treasure Island, Oakland, Berkeley, and continuing to Mare Island Naval Shipyard, where their voyage would end.

Sailors and Marines packed their bags and went topside again to watch the sights. At the pier in Mare Island, crowds of sailors and family members cheered and waved in expectation of their reunions. A small Navy Band played Anchors Aweigh, the Navy Hymn, and other welcome home tunes. Docking a large ship using tugboats can take an hour, and the wait was frustratingly long for the anxious servicemen waiting to disembark and get on dry land again.

After the normal military routine of "Hurry up and wait," Clyde could finally disembark and get off the pier. He located his assigned barracks and began searching for an available pay phone with the shortest line. Three thousand plus servicemen were trying to call families at the same time. After an hour in line, he gave up in favor of trying to buy a train ticket to Chicago as soon as possible. Train tickets for servicemen were available at the base United Service Organizations (USO) office. There, one could also send a Western Union telegram or V-Mail-gram (photo-fax type) free of charge. But to whom and where should he send it? His gal could be anywhere in Northern Illinois. "Address the telegram to Shirley Hennings, Antioch, Illinois. It's a small

16

town, and everyone knows everyone; they'll know the address." Clyde told the telegraph operator.

The operator read the message back out loud. *"Arrived California 30 July. STOP. Will advise arrival in Chicago soon. STOP Clyde. STOP."*

Clyde nodded his head in agreement.

"Okay, sailor, this should go out in tonight's batch. That'll be Fifty Cents, please," replied the operator. Clyde asked about eastbound train schedules. "Probably won't get out until tomorrow night's eastbound at 1900 hours. The servicemen's rate is thirty dollars to Chicago, including transfers at Ogden, Utah, and Cheyenne, Wyoming. It takes three nights and three days to Chicago," said the operator as Clyde dug through his wallet for the cash.

After dinner in the Mess Hall, Clyde went back to the barracks. Thinking to himself - "Am I really ready to do this - Get married?" Then he remembered all the letters and gifts he sent Shirley. "You bet I am…." As he laid back on his bunk, as the memories of Boot Camp came flooding back.

Two - Recruits

July 1942. Standing outside the Naval Recruiting Office in Akron, Ohio, it was very hot, nearly 100 degrees, and nearly 100 percent humidity. The recruits moved slowly in the hot afternoon sun as the line snaked out the front door and around the corner. Once inside, they were taken in groups of one hundred for processing. First, more forms would be filled out, then off to the swearing-in ceremony.

"Raise your right hand," shouted the Chief Petty Officer. "Do you swear... ...So help me God, I do." The Chief paused for effect. "Now, you boys are in the Navy, and we'll make sailors out of you. Get down the hall, strip down to your jockey shorts, and get in line for your physicals. That number you're holding is your number until you arrive at the Great Lake Training Center. Now get out of here! On the double!"

After the swearing-in ceremony, two nervous recruits were standing in line waiting to be processed by a doctor. Clyde was number 117, and 118 was a stranger named Harold.

"Well, I see we are going to be pretty close for a while. I'm Harold Jensen from Akron."

"Hi, I'm Clyde McLain from Uniontown. Glad to meet you. What do you want to do in the Navy?"

"Anything. Being a gas pump jockey is the pits. I've had two jobs that paid twenty cents an hour. A guy just can't make it on that. They say the Navy is good duty and pay is okay too, and it's better than walking everywhere carrying a rifle!" Harold admitted with a smile.

Clyde shook his head in agreement. "Yeah, you're right. I heard they needed machinists really bad, and I need steady pay, too. Been working at Goodyear Tire Company as an apprentice machinist. My chances of making Journeyman at Goodyear are almost zero. Maybe I can get ahead in the Navy. And besides, I'd like to help kill some of those damned Japanese or Germans."

"You're right; winning the war is the main thing, and shooting those big guns at the enemy could be a real swell time." Harold grinned.

Clyde shivered and said, "I wish this line would move up a little faster; I'm getting cold standing here in my skivvies."

"Clyde, they just called our numbers. Wow! look at that pretty nurse!" Harold smiled.

"Yeah, she's a knockout! And look at that huge needle the doctor has! I'm feeling sick," said Clyde.

"Oh, come on, Clyde, you don't want to pass out in the middle of the physical exam do you? You could be kicked out of the Navy. Pull yourself together!"

"Number 117 Next!" the doctor shouted. Clyde stepped up in front of the doc who shouted out the orders. "Cough. Take a deep breath. Now, let it out. Read the eye chart. Let me check your feet. Over here to listen to your heart. Now give me that right shoulder." Ka-zap went the hypodermic gun with that big needle. "You pass. Move along" as the doctor pointed down the hall he shouted, "Number 118 next!"

After dressing, they gathered their personal gear and went outside. All the recruits boarded a bus to the train station where the next troop train transported them to the US Naval Training Center, Great Lakes, near Chicago, Illinois. For the next six months, that would be home to these Ohio boys.

Thirty-six hours later, Harold and Clyde and thousands of other recruits arrived at Great Lakes Naval Training Center. Most had never been this far from their hometowns in their lives.

"Wow, have you ever seen such tall buildings? Look at that train up in the air. Where's its steam engine?" asked Harold.

"It's an electric trolly but up above the street traffic," Clyde responded. "Maybe we'll get some leave time to do some sightseeing and ride that fancy trolly."

The train slowed to a stop inside Great Lakes Naval Base. The whistle blew to signal it was time to disembark.

Clyde and Harold grabbed their bags and stepped off the train, only to be greeted by the Chief Petty Officer Drill Instructor shouting, "Hurry up, you sorry, lazy bums, it's time to make sailors out of you worthless-no-good scumbags. Fall-in over here. Hurry up, I ain't got all day! Get on those buses and stow your gear on top. Hurry up! We got another train waiting to unload. Let's go, you sorry sons of bitches, you're in the Navy now!"

Back in his Mare Island bunk, Clyde said to himself, "Wow, that was almost three years ago. A world away and a beginning of a new adventure." The bugler blew Tattoo and Taps over the base loudspeakers. The bunkhouse was quiet, with lights out at 2200 hours.

Three - Sweet Friends

Fall 1942. It was a lazy, quiet afternoon at *Ted's Sweet Shop* in Antioch, Illinois, and a fall chill was in the air. Suddenly, Betty Hanké burst through the glass door as its bell rang loudly and announced her presence. "Hi, Shirley!" Betty was always a neatly dressed young woman, a thoroughly modern woman of twenty-one years. She worked as an office secretary at the *Pickard China* factory in Antioch and was trained on the elite '*IBM punch card machine.*'

Shirley Hennings emerged from the back room of *Ted's Sweet Shop*, where she worked on her days off. "Hi, Bets. How you gettin' along today?"

"Doing better today. Went back to work. What's new with you?" Betty had been recovering from a cold over the weekend.

"That's good. Glad to hear it. Can I get you something?" Shirley replied.

"How's the rocky road ice cream today?" Betty inquired.

"Sorry dearie, but we've been out of it all week. Can't get any from the creamery because their allotment of milk for the war effort has shut down ice-cream production for a few days. Maybe next week it'll be better," Shirley explained.

"Okay. Ah…how about a chocolate soda instead?" Bets sat down on the round stool at the soda counter.

Shirley started making the soda, adding a squirt of chocolate syrup to a cup of ice. Next, a jerk on the soda fountain handle for some carbonated water over the ice. Anxious to pass on some of the daily gossip, she said, "Hey, did you hear about Bud Brown? He got his draft notice this week. He'll be leaving in a few days." She handed the chocolate soda to Bets.

"Well, I'll be…! That's another dreamy hunk out of commission for the duration," Betty said as she sighed sadly.

"Oh well, we'll just have to go to the Aragon Ballroom in Chicago this weekend and cry a few tears. I hear it's overflowing with great-looking soldiers and sailors ready for a fun time. Say, we could also spend the day shopping at Marshall Field's department store." A smile came over Shirley's face as she thought about a night out in Chicago.

"Yeah, Shirl, a man in uniform is so irresistible. Those cute bell-bottom pants and silk ties on the sailors are all right by me. You know how naughty sailors are, or at least that's what I've heard." Betty's spirits brightened up. The two young women looked at each other, giggling, and smiled briefly.

"I have my dress design class in the city on Thursday afternoon, so call me at grandma's house that evening, and we'll make our plans for the weekend." Shirley had been attending classes on dress design at the local Chicago Designer school inside the Chicago Loop.

"Well, Shirsh, gotta run! Gotta get to the Piggly-Wiggly before dinner. Gotta bring home some sugar for Mom. She's making a cake for the Methodist Women on Sunday. I've got her ration card to buy some." Bets finished her chocolate soda, left a nickel on the counter, and hurried out the door.

"Call me later!" Shirley shouted as Betty walked through the door with the bell ringing. Shirley laughed and returned to helping her brother-in-law, Ted, make candy in the back room.

"Who was that?" asked Ted as he brought out a tray of chocolate-covered nougats.

"Just Bets. She was on her way to the Piggly-Wiggly. Just stopped in to say 'Hi' and get a soda." Shirley continued, "When will we get some Rocky Road in? That's her favorite."

"Not sure," Ted replied. "I hope we can get enough sugar so I can make candy canes for Christmas. With this war, we never know what's going to be available." He sighed, "Just like in the Old Country, we never had the basic foods or the money to buy them. It's still better in this New Country." [1]

---

[1] Theodore Poulos, or Ted for short, had made his best-selling hand-dipped chocolate bonbons since 1928. He made a lot of different kinds of candy, including hand-pulled taffy and hand-twisted candy canes for Christmas, and even the very special hand-decorated white chocolate Easter Eggs filled with candied fruit, made in the traditional Greek way. Ted's hand-made candies were famous throughout northern Illinois and southern Wisconsin. Ted came to America from Greece in 1914 and

immediately went to work at the ore smelter in McGill, Nevada. His sister and brother-in-law sponsored his emigration. Like many young Greeks, Ted hoped to escape the poor economy in his homeland and the threats of war in Europe. During the Depression, he learned the art of candy making from Greeks in Logan, Utah. Ted stayed close to Greek communities and eventually moved to Chicago, home of the largest Greek community in the United States. He married Shirley's eldest sister, Phyllis, in the Chicago Greek Orthodox church in 1932, and they had two sons, Peter and Thomas. Phyllis died very shortly after Thomas was born. Shirley took care of Ted's boys while in high school and helped him with the soda fountain and the candy shop whenever she had time. Ted never remarried and always remained a full member of Shirley's family.

Four - On the train

31 July, 1945. "Hurry up, sailor, you're going to miss the bus to the train station!" the bus driver shouted. "I'm coming, don't want to miss the train. Gotta see my girl in Chicago!" Clyde struggled to hurry under the weight of his seabag over his shoulder. "How far is the train station?" He got on the bus as the driver closed the door.

The driver said, "We're going to the Union Pacific station in Martinez on the other side of the Vallejo bridge. There's lots of traffic on the way. Lots of soldiers and sailors have been on leave since VE Day. Lots of troops moving in and out. We gotta hurry, or everyone will miss the eastbound train." The bus chugged away from the base with its heavy load of sailors.

"There are seats in the next car, sailor; your bag goes on that hand cart. Here's a tag. Bags will be loaded and transferred to the Chicago train in Cheyenne. These last cars go all the way to Chicago," said the Steward. "Thanks," Clyde replied and climbed up the steps. He found an empty seat and relaxed for a few minutes. The train whistle blew, and the train lurched forward to start its long journey eastward.

"Hey sailor, what's your name? I'm Joe, heading for Milwaukee," said a Marine sitting across from Clyde.

"Hi, I'm Clyde. Chicago is my destination. Where's your unit?"

The sergeant replied, "Got a lottery ticket out for a 30-day leave. My first break since early '43. After the war in Europe was over, some of us caught a break after Okinawa. They started rotating us out for a little R&R. My unit is moving on with some fresh troops coming up from the rear. That's been one hell of a battle. Where's your unit?"

Clyde said, "Been in Pearl Harbor since '43 working on submarine repairs in the Machine Shop. It was a mess after the attack. Had to keep those fleet boats running so they can strangle the Japanese shipping and stop ToJo."

"Did you see which way the canteen was? I'm getting hungry," Joe asked.

"I think it was about three cars forward. Good luck getting something to eat," replied Clyde with a chuckle.

The next evening, the train stopped in Ogden, Utah. The car steward announced, "There is a two-hour layover in the station to refuel and take on more supplies."

Clyde got off the train and looked for the Western Union Telegram office in the train station. *"Ogden UT 803 PM 1 August Miss Shirley Hennings Antioch Ill STOP Arrive Furlough Challenger C&NW Station 9:20 AM Friday STOP Love Clyde McLain STOP,* that'll be Sixty-five cents today," said the telegram clerk.

Clyde walked back to the train with a coffee from the USO canteen. "Looks like folks are pretty busy around here," Clyde said to a station attendant.

"Oh yes, sir. We are always busy. This is a major connection for trains in all directions. Why, we have over one hundred trains every day coming through here since the war began. It's gotten heavier since the war in Europe is over. Soldiers from Europe are going to the Pacific, along with all their equipment." The attendant waved, "Gotta run. Good luck."

"All aboard!" shouted the Conductor as the train rolled out of the station. Clyde settled into his seat and remembered the incredible views of New Mexico and the Rocky Mountains on his first trip west.[2] Clyde commented to the soldier sitting near him, "It's going to be hot today, maybe a hundred and five."

"Yeah," said the soldier, wiping his brow. "But not as hot as those Pacific islands I've been fightin' on. A hundred and ten and a hundred percent humidity. You could never get a break from the heat, even if the bullets weren't flying overhead."

As Clyde wiped his brow, he remembered how hot it had been in Hawaii and how he wished for some cooler weather. He remembered his last days in Chicago: Harold and Clyde had been in the Great Lakes Naval Training Center since the warm days of July 1942. Then Clyde recalled the first snows in Chicago; how the north wind blew

---

[2]Troop trains always get priority on the railroads. The westbound train went through Illinois, Iowa, Nebraska, Dodge City, Kansas, Albuquerque, Grants, Gallup, New Mexico, Flagstaff, Kingman, Arizona, Needles, Sierra-Nevada mountains, San Fernando Valley, and Oakland California. The scenery was great. Hoping to see some more incredible scenes on the return. The eastbound Furlough Challenger was a special Chicago & North Western train traveling on the old "City of San Francisco" route shared by the Union Pacific Railroad from Oakland, over the Sierra mountains, to Ogden, Cheyenne, Omaha, to Chicago.

through the Training Center to Lake Michigan with a vengeance, when the wind chill temperatures would drop into the minus twenty degrees. The dark blue wool Navy uniform helped some, but the heavy Navy Peacoat was an absolute must just to venture outside. They had finished their boot camp training and nearly finished their machinist school. With a twenty-four-hour Liberty Pass, a sailor could take a day off for sightseeing around Chicago. However, "Oh boy, it's cold outside" was the word of the day.

Five - The Invitation

Mid-December 1942. Winds gusted between the buildings of downtown Chicago as Betty Hanké ran toward the train station, hoping to catch the afternoon train to Antioch. With her packages in tow and somewhat disheveled, she stops at the platform to straighten herself and her hair before stepping onto the train platform. The northbound Great Northern train was preparing to leave the station. She heard the conductor call, "All aboard!" She quickly grabbed her packages tighter and stepped aboard the waiting coach. The Saturday afternoon train was crowded with Christmas shoppers.

"Here, take my seat, Miss." Harold jumped up and offered his seat to the nicely dressed young woman. He was wearing his US Navy dress blue uniform and white hat, and was returning to base after a day of sightseeing in Chicago.

"Oh, why thank you, sir. Are you returning to the Great Lakes?" Betty inquired.

"Yes, Ma'am, I am. Got a day pass to see the city before our final exams next week," he replied, hoping to continue the conversation, "And you? Where are you heading?"

"Home to Antioch. I've been with a friend at Marshall Fields. It's a big department store on State Street inside the Loop," Betty replied as she stored her packages under her seat.

"Looks like you've been shopping for Christmas before it gets too late, huh?" Harold ventured a guess, eyeing her packages.

"Oh yeah. Had to get a few things in the mail for my two brothers in the Army in Europe. It takes two or three weeks to get the smallest things there, and I want their gifts to arrive by Christmas Day." She sighed in sadness at the thought of not having her brothers at home for the holidays.

"I think our class will ship out after Christmas. We don't know where we are going to be stationed yet, but the Navy needs lots of ships in the Pacific," Harold suggested.

Betty eyed the neatly dressed-looking sailor and smiled as she asked, "Where's 'home' sailor?"

"Akron, Ohio. My name is Harold Jensen. I've been at Great Lakes since last July with basic and advanced machinist training. May I ask your name, miss?"

"I'm Betty Hanké from Antioch. It's a small town about twenty miles north of Chicago," she replied. "I wonder if we'll get a white Christmas this year?"

"It would be swell if we did. But it's not much of a holiday on the base anyway without your family and just the same old smelly guys to look at. I'm really looking forward to getting on a train to anywhere. Just thinking about January in Chicago makes me want to go to Hawaii or somewhere warm." Harold lamented.

As the train slowed, the Conductor called out, "Next stop, Great Lakes Naval Base."

"Oh, darn, this is my station. I'll have to say 'goodbye,' and I wish you a very merry Christmas." With that, Harold stood up and nodded to the pretty young woman on the train.

Betty finished writing on a piece of paper, and handed it to Harold and said, "If you get a pass for Christmas, give me a call for dinner. Mother's making dinner and having a serviceman joining us would be nice. My brothers can't come home, but I know mom would like to hear a little masculine talk for a change. Here is the phone number and address."

"Thank you very kindly, Miss Betty; I doubt I'll get a pass, but if I do, you'll be the first one I'll call." Harold smiled very widely and took the note. As he stepped onto the platform, he wondered: was this a dream or for real? Harold clutched the note as the train whistled and rolled down the tracks. He smiled quietly and thought, "She's the 'Cat's Meow.' Don't lose that note!"

23 December 1942. "It won't be long now. In a few weeks, we'll be graduating," Clyde said.

"Can't wait. I'm sick of the Great Lakes, Chicago, and the whole mess here. Nothing good's going on. We take the final machinist exam on Monday, but graduation's not for a month. Mid-January, I think." Harold sighed.

"Do you think we'll get liberty for Christmas? I could sure use some time to get away. I haven't been home to see Mom since June. You got any plans?" Clyde asked.

"Oh, I don't know. I met this gal on the train the other day, coming back from Chicago. She has a couple of brothers in the Army, and she gave me her number and address and said I was invited for Christmas dinner. I don't know, but she was very nice-looking and had a sweet voice." Harold smiled as he remembered her conversation. "I don't have a clue where Antioch is. What do you think? Want to come along?"

Clyde thought about it for a moment. "Well, it sounds fine to me, but I don't want to be cuttin' in on your date or anything like that."

"Oh, I don't think we are a 'thing' yet. Just met her. But I could use some home-cooked food for the holidays. Anything but this Navy mess hall slop," Harold said.

"Well, if you put it that way, count me in. Besides, we probably won't get a pass for Christmas day anyway," Clyde replied.

Six - The Christmas Dinner

25 December 1942. Christmas Day started with a snowstorm, and the holiday travelers were slowed to almost a complete stop. "Gee, Harold, it's snowing to beat the band. Are you sure you're going to dinner with that girl from the train?" Clyde shook his head in disbelief.

"Her name is Betty, and I'm not going to let a little snow stop me from seeing her again and getting a home-cooked meal. I have had enough of that SOS slop in the mess hall. And," Harold paused, "You're going with me! No arguments! You can't just sit here by yourself on Christmas Day. Grab your peacoat and gloves, and let's see if we can make the train in time."

With Liberty passes in hand, the two bunkmates double-timed it to the train station in Great Lakes. "Damn, the last train has gone already!" Harold said, exhausted from the trek. "Come on, we're only fifteen miles away. We can hitch a ride to Antioch and be there by dinner." The two sailors hurried off to the highway. They buttoned up their peacoat and pulled their hats down tight to keep them from blowing off. The two sailors, with their dark blue uniforms and thumbs held high, must have looked like twin *Statues of Liberty* in the sea of white snow.

They watched as the first couple of cars passed by and didn't stop. Then, a 1938 Ford sedan pulled over, and the elderly driver asked, "Where you boys going?"

"Antioch, sir. Or as far as you can take us," came the reply from Harold.

"Okay. Hop in. That's where I'm going." In a few seconds, the cold sailors were seated and trying to warm up from the blustery Cook County weather. "Hi, I'm Nicholas Licopoulos. They call me Doctor Nick. What's your name and where are you from?" With that, the driver sped away onto the snow-covered road.

"I'm Harold from Akron," "I'm Clyde from Uniontown near Akron," the two young men replied.

"Weather forecast is for about eight inches of snow tonight. You're lucky I saw you, fellas, in this snowstorm. Let me guess; you two are going to meet some gals with your dress blues on and hitching a ride in a storm. Am I right?" Dr. Nick said.

"Is it that obvious?" Harold replied.

"No sailor would go to Antioch, Illinois unless he had a lady friend. So, who is she? It's a small town, and everybody knows everyone."

"Her name is Betty Hanké. Do you know her family?" Harold said quietly, as if not wanting to give away his secret.

"Betty Hanké! I know the family well! Delivered all those kids, including 'Bets.' Her father died in either 36 or 37 in a car accident." The excitement in Doc's voice raised as he continued, "I know exactly where they live. I'll be glad to drop you boys off at their front door if the road's not too bad and the weather doesn't get much worse."

Harold looked at Clyde as if to say, "Is this really happening?" Then, they settled back for a warm ride to the town of Antioch. In about 35 minutes, they arrived at the Hanké house unannounced. It was about 3:30 PM.

"I hope you know what you're going to say before you ring the doorbell," Clyde told Harold. "This could get really embarrassing for everyone."

"I got it handled. Don't worry." Harold said as he pressed the buzzer on the doorpost.

The door opened narrowly to keep out the cold. Harold stuttered, "Ah, hello. I'm Harold Jensen, and I am here to see Betty. Please."

"One moment. Betty! Someone here to see you," the voice called from inside.

Then the gal of the hour appeared at the door with a look of total surprise, aghast with shock. "Ah, hi." Betty wondered who are these shivering sailors.

"Hi Betty, I'm Harold Jensen from the train last week. You gave me your address and said to stop by for a while if I got a Liberty Pass. Well, I did, and I kept your note. I hope you don't mind, but I brought Clyde McLain along with me because he was just sitting in the barracks alone."

"Ah, yes, I remember. Certainly, it's alright to bring your friend along on this Christmas Day. Come on in and get warm. Shake off the snow from our coats and hang them over there. Have a seat in the parlor room," Betty said shyly and nervously.

Betty ran into the kitchen and exclaimed to Nellie, "Mom, we've got two more mouths to feed for dinner. A sailor that I met in Chicago and brought his buddy along. Do we have enough for them too?"

Nellie smiled and replied, "We'll make do, my dear. I used all our ration coupons this week to get what we needed for dinner. We can add some water to the soup and cut the ham a little thinner and cut the cake smaller, too." She paused. "And it would be just like Allen and Leslie[3] were home with us from the Army tonight, sitting around our table. Please welcome our servicemen into our home, Dear."

"Please come in and make yourself at home," Betty said, motioning the sailors into the front parlor room.

The 1920s Sears and Roebuck house on Bishop Street was decorated in the 1942 "blackout" style of the period. No festive lights. A modest wreath on the door. The heavy blackout window curtains were closed to keep the light and heat inside. But inside, there was the traditional Christmas tree: a small local cedar tree, less than four feet tall, covered with glass ornaments from years ago, and a new string of popcorn garland wound very carefully from side to side. And the glass angel on top. Only a few small electric lights were placed in strategic locations.

"Have a seat. Hi, I'm Betty Hanké, and we haven't met yet," she said, holding her hand to Clyde.

------

[3] Allen Hanké, Betty's oldest brother, died during the Battle of the Bulge in December 1944. Leslie Hanké was injured by shrapnel in early 1945 in Europe. Leslie (Les) walked with a limp, having lost part of his foot from a land mine. He returned home in 1945 and became a local butcher in Antioch.

"Ah. Hi, I'm Clyde McLain, from Akron, Ohio, from the U.S. Navy in the Great Lakes Training Center. Very pleased to meet you, miss. You have such a beautiful home; I hope I am not putting you folks out. Harold asked me to come along, and he just wouldn't take "no" for an answer." And then he sat down.

Betty was curious between the blackout orders and the snowstorm: "Tell me, Harold, how on earth did you find this place in the middle of this snowstorm?"

"Well, you won't believe this, but we were picked up outside of Waukegan by your very own Doctor Nick! He knew just where to go." He paused. "I don't know how we will get back to base again," Harold replied whimsically. "We missed the train and started hitchin' a ride. Then he came along. I hope we're not intruding. I would have called, but the base pay phones had been so busy with sailors calling home that we couldn't get through to call you. And we didn't have enough change to make a person-to-person call. Then we thought we could just get on the train and be here in a short time."

"Oh, that's fine. Mom and I are alone tonight for Christmas. My two brothers, Allen and Leslie, are gone in the Army, and it is nice to have you two sailors here to stand in for them," Betty said with a tear in her eye. "They are off somewhere in England or Northern Africa. Allen is in the 3rd Armored Division, driving a tank. Leslie is in the Infantry. We don't get a lot of mail from them, and when they write, they can't say much. So 'no news is good news' the way we figure it. What's on the horizon for you guys?"

"We're supposed to graduate from Great Lakes in the middle of January and be shipped out to God-knows-where.

The Navy never tells you anything until the last minute, and then you still have to wait to see what really happens," Harold replied, "Clyde and I have been in school for eighteen weeks, and after Basic Training, we've been studying in the machinist school. Clyde's an excellent machinist. We met in Akron when we signed up. Clyde requested machinist school, and I thought that sounded better than artillery. We've been together since we signed up. It was either be drafted and get assigned to a job we didn't want or sign up and choose what we are good at."

"What a minute," Clyde protested. "I'm not an expert, just an apprentice machinist who worked at Goodyear Tire and Rubber Company before signing up with the Navy. Journeyman machinist jobs are very scarce, and my chances of making journeyman were pretty slim. So, I signed up to make some more money for the family back in Ohio and West Virginia."

"I thought you said you were from Akron, not West Virginia?" Betty remarked inquisitively, thinking she heard wrong.

"Well, my family home is in Parkersburg, West 'By-God' Virginia. After graduating in 1938 from high school, I moved to Uniontown, Ohio, near Akron, and lived and worked with my aunt and uncle on their poultry farm. They needed help, and a young man fresh from school needed a job so he could help out his family. During the 30s, I had a paper route, the only money my family had because times were tough in West Virginia. Almost half the men were out of work from the Depression."

"In 1940, my uncle got word of an apprentice program beginning at Goodyear. I applied and was put on the waiting list. Before their classes began, several students dropped out, and I got the last seat open. Pure luck." Clyde reflected on his experience at Goodyear. "I was good with math in high school, and it paid off in the apprentice program. I hope I did well in the Navy program. It's been pretty tough."

"Well, you boys, just relax here and warm up while I go see if I can help Mom with the meal. Can I get you anything to drink? We only have water and home-squeezed lemonade. The ration coupons didn't allow us to get any extra milk this week. Already used up our allotments baking the cake and Christmas cookies," Betty said as she got up and left the room.

With Harold and Clyde settled in, Betty quietly talked to Nellie in the kitchen. "Mom, what am I going to do? Harold came to visit me, and this other guy came along, too. I can't keep two sailors talking all night and help you out, too. What should I do?"

"Why don't you call Shirley? You two do everything together, and she's like family. And, what's one more mouth to feed tonight?" Nellie said, wanting to help her daughter out of her dilemma.

"Great idea! Her family is so big they won't even know she's gone." Betty said as she picked up the phone and clicked the receiver. The operator came on the line, "Number, please?" "Oh, hi, Hattie. Would you connect me to the Hennings' home, please? And Merry Christmas to you." "Connecting." "Hi, Leona. Can I speak to Shirley?" A few moments later, a voice came on the line, "Hi, Bets, Merry Christmas, what's goin' on?"

"Oh, Shirsh! I'm in big trouble! I invited a sailor to dinner last week, just to be polite, and he is kind of cute. But hold me back! He comes and shows up at the door tonight and with his buddy!" Betty exclaimed. "I really need your help. You need to come over and get me out of this jam. Excuse yourself from dinner, and come over and join us. Mom suggested it! It'll be great fun. What do you say?"

"Wow, sounds like you got in big trouble. Is the other guy cute?" Shirley shot back. "Okay, I'll check with my mom. Hang on a minute." The line went quiet for a few moments, then she returned. "Okay. I think that my brother-in-law Einar will drive me over. We'll be there in about twenty minutes. Can I bring something for dinner? Okay. See ya."[4]

At the Hennings house, it was pandemonium in preparation for Christmas dinner. There were six daughters born to C.E. and Sophie. Four were married, and Shirley and her younger sister were single. The children, about fifteen in 1942, were running and playing at full volume and full of

---

[4] Shirley's family was large compared to Betty's. There was her father, Courtly Everest Hennings, and mother, Sophia, or "Sophie," as their friends referred to her. Sophie was born in San Francisco, California 1898, and was the firstborn of Greek immigrants and carried a strong Greek influence into the family. Courtly, called "C.E." by almost everyone, ran the newspaper business in the Lake County area. He employed several family members to drive the delivery trucks and process the papers and bills. During the Depression Era, newspapers were the "internet" of the 1930s and 1940s. Even the very poor needed to have a penny to buy a paper to find a job or to buy and sell their wares. The Hennings family would be considered wealthy by 1940 standards. Daily newspaper delivery was a critical resource to the country, and C.E. needed lots of fuel to deliver his papers. Shirley often drove the Chevrolet panel trucks to help the business in the late 30s and 40s.

energy. The whole family was there helping to finish the decorating and preparing Christmas dinner. Evelyn, sister number four, was arriving with Ed and their three children, bringing gifts and food to share.

Shirley asked to be excused so she could help out Betty Hanké. Sophie, who ruled the house, laughed at her predicament and said, "Get out of here and have fun! Get Einar to drive you over; he's just sitting there smoking that big cigar. Give him something to do," as she went back to the kitchen.

Einar, a big red-headed Swede who had married Shirley's second sister, Leona, drove the daily paper truck for the daily business and was used to driving in the heavy snows of northern Illinois. He grumbled a little at getting up from the card game to go outside in the cold weather. Einar's brother, Nels, had married Shirley's third sister, Elaine, and were always trying to beat their father-in-law in their daily card games of Rummy. Soon, Shirley and Einar were off to the Bishop Street house.

"Hi, Shirl, come on in. So glad you're here. We're all in the living room." The two sailors stood up as the two women entered the room, waiting to be introduced. "This is Shirley Hennings. My best friend. Shirley, this is Harold Jensen and Clyde McLain. They are from the Great Lakes Naval Base."

"Hello. Very pleased to meet you," the two young men said almost simultaneously as they shook hands and sat down. An awkward silence set in as each person tried to start the conversation. The silence was broken by the sounds of Bing Crosby singing his new hit song, *White Christmas*, on the radio. The smells of dinner wafted throughout the house.

As the conversations began, Nellie called them to the dinner table. The smells had heightened their appetites, and the group jumped at the chance to enjoy the meal. The meal conversations were pleasant and varied as the guests were at the table. The sailors continued to praise how much better the delicious home-cooked food tasted, meager as it was when compared to six months of Navy chow.

After dinner, Betty said, "Have you seen that new movie *The Black Swan* with Tyrone Power and Maureen O'Hara?"

"No," replied Harold.

"Well, it's playing at the theater in Kenosha, Wisconsin. The show starts at 7:30. It would be lots of fun. Want to go?" Betty replied. "Tyrone is a real hunk, and Maureen is a dish. It'll be a swell time."

"You could take Allen's car. It's just sitting here while he's in the Army. That's IF it starts," Nellie suggested.

"What a great idea! I can get a few gallons of gas from our newspaper trucks, so you won't have to use up your ration coupons," Shirley said. "Come on. Shake a leg, and let's get going. It'll be fun." And the foursome grabbed their coats and hats and headed out to see if they could start the old Ford.

The weather was clearing up, and the snow had stopped. In some places, it had melted with the help of salt applied to the main roads and highways. The gang of four headed off to the theater in Kenosha, Wisconsin, about ten miles north of Antioch, which is one mile from the state line. The old Ford ran well with new gas, but with four people inside and 30-32 degrees outside, the car's windows were completely fogged over. If the car had a heater, it still wasn't very warm.

The cold air didn't stall the usual conversations about what's in and out, who's doing what, and your plans for the future. The laughter and jokes were just as 'corny' as their popcorn in the theater. Movies were one the most important news sources of the 30s and 40s, like the newspapers and radio. The short current event newsreels gave hometown folks a look into the outside world, especially the war and its devastation. Those young sailors paid particular attention as they watched the newsreel reports on the naval battles at Guadalcanal and the South Pacific campaigns, into which they would be going in the next few months.

After the movie, the group found an ice cream shop next to the theater. And reviews of the movie were glowing. They all agreed on how beautiful Maureen O'Hara looked and how dashing and debonaire Tyrone Power was. As they jumped back in the car to head back to Antioch, someone looked at the time.

"We've missed the last train back to Great Lakes. What should we do to get you guys back to base?" Betty said. "What time do you need to be back on base?"

"Our passes are up at midnight. We better get hitchhiking and start walking," Harold said. "We've got just over two hours."

Shirley piped up, "I'll get us some gas, and we'll drive you guys home."

Betty agreed to the plan. "Yeah, sounds great. The roads are much better now, but we still have to drive 25 to 30 miles per hour. But we should get you there on time."

And off they went, heading south on the state highway. With the temperatures falling, the conversation on the way back to base was just as fast and lively as during the drive north, almost never a quiet moment. Clyde and Shirley, riding in the backseat, snuggled a little tighter to stave off the frigid air.

As the car pulled up to the gate at Great Lakes, the couples exchanged addresses and telephone numbers. "Well, here you guys are," Betty said with a bit of sadness. "It's been just a swell time."

"Please tell Nellie how much we enjoyed the Christmas dinner and all of her hard work and sacrifice," Harold said, smiling. "Betty, thanks for inviting me."

"You mean *US*." Clyde corrected him. "Thank you so much. And thank you for inviting your lovely friend Shirley to join us." Clyde turned to Shirley and whispered, "I'll call you tomorrow evening if I can get a break from work. I'd like to see you again."

With their 'goodbyes' over, the sailors straightened their hats and ties and exited the car. Shouts of "See you later." were heard by the sentries at the gate as the sailors saluted and passed through the gate. It was quarter to twelve as they hurried off to the barracks.

Betty drove Shirley to her grandmother's house on Parkside Avenue in Chicago. Betty smiled and said, "Well, you and Clyde sure hit it off pretty well. I'd think you were life-long friends." "Harold was nice but quiet. It's hard to know what he was thinking."

Shirley grinned and giggled a little. "I don't know what got into me, but that West Virginia guy was something really special. He was swell."

"Did you two make any plans for another date?" Betty wondered.

"Not really, but he said he would call when he had time." Shirley hoped.

"Harold and I didn't make definite plans either. I never quite know what he's thinking. A bit overwhelming for him, I guess," Betty replied.

"Here's my grandma's house. It's been a great evening. Thanks for inviting me, I'll never forget it. I can't wait to tell Granny all about it. Call me tomorrow. Love you. Merry Christmas!" The two women hugged each other and waved as the car pulled away. Shirley fumbled for her key to the house when Grandma Lila Dahl opened the door and welcomed her in from the cold night air.

Saturday 26 December. The next afternoon, the phone rang, and Shirley ran to answer it.

"Hi, may I speak with Shirley, please?" said the voice on the phone.

"Hi, this is Shirley," she replied.

"This is Clyde. How are you today? Guess you gals got home safely without any problems?" Clyde inquired.

"O yeah, we got home okay. How are you today?" Shirley asked.

"Doing great. Ah, say, we, that is Harold and I, were talking about all the fun we had last night and thought, ah, maybe you and Bets could meet us in Chicago. Anyway, I was just hoping that you might have some free time this evening or Sunday to see the city and maybe get a bite to eat. I'm off after 4:30 today." Clyde asks with a little fear and trembling.

"Are you asking me out on a date?" she asked, holding her breath.

"Well, yes, I guess I am. What do you say? Can we make it a date?" Clyde replied nervously. "Could you call Betty and see if she could come along? Harold lost her phone number."

"I'd love to Clyde, but tonight I was planning to go with granny to the Chicago Theater. I already have the tickets. But on Sunday I'm free after church. Will that work?" Shirley proposed. "I'll call Bets and see what she's doing."

"Yeah, sure. It'll be a swell time. What time and where can we meet?" Clyde replied excitedly. They both had to take a bus to the center of the city, so they decided where to meet.

"See you tomorrow." She hung up the telephone and yelled, "Hey grandma, you won't believe…." And started to excitedly recite what had just taken place.

Shirley dialed the phone. "Hey, Bets, you want to get together with Clyde and Harold tomorrow in Chicago? It'll be fun. He suggested a little dinner and some sightseeing around the Loop. What'd you say?"

"You sure had a swell time with Clyde, but I'm not sure Harold had as much fun," Betty replied. "Oh, why not? I can't resist a man in uniform. Hal was pretty nice. Maybe overwhelmed with all of it. Sure, I'll call you back in a few minutes." And she hung up the phone.

27 December. Sunday started out like usual: breakfast with Grandma, off to church, and back by noon. The excitement was overflowing into everything Shirley did. "Got to get going; the bus will be here soon. I'll call you later when I know what we are doing," she said as she put on her hat, coat, gloves, and rubber galoshes (boots). The winter weather had returned, and the "windy city" was living up to its name. But even a sailor would be hard-pressed to see her nicest dress and necklace under all those winter clothes.

Shirley arrived early at the corner of South Michigan and West Madison streets, where the bus let her off. They were all going to meet there. Bets arrived about five minutes later. The bus from Great Lakes let the two sailors off a few blocks north of the women. The sailors walked as fast as they could to keep warm and reach the gals without delay. The gang greeted each other within ten minutes, laughing and talking fast and loudly. What excitement and anticipation filled the air, hoping to recreate the memories from Christmas day.

"First, where can we get a cup of coffee to warm up a little? My teeth are chattering, and I'm frozen. These sailor suits and peacoats aren't the warmest things in the world," Harold said, shaking like a leaf.

"In the next block, I know a coffee shop that should be open," Shirley suggested.

The bell on the door jingled when they entered the shop. Everyone was ready for something warm. Coffee hit the spot.

"Where do you ladies want to go for dinner?" Clyde asked.

"How about going past the Water Tower and up Rush Street? There are a few small restaurants and a few places to dance," Shirley suggested since she was currently living in the "City" and therefore considered an expert guide. They walked past the Chicago River and up Michigan Avenue. The wind howled between the buildings, but no one seemed to care, especially Clyde and Shirley, locked arm-in-arm to keep warm as they walked briskly down the snow-covered streets.

Shirley said, "This little Italian place downstairs should be alright. There is no cover charge, the food is passible, and they have a dance floor and music. The band is probably not playing tonight, but they have records all the time."

The foursome didn't waste much time finding a table and settling in for a warm meal. Hopefully, it's not too expensive for sailors on a meager income. Christmas songs were still playing, mixed in between the current dance favorites of the day. Dancing was the hit of the evening, even if the two Ohio boys didn't know their left foot from their right. The gals just laughed at the 'country bumpkins.' The best time was those slow dances that everyone loved. Her perfume and his shaving cologne. Soft music. Good food. It was a heavenly evening.

"Whoa, we better get going! The last bus for Great Lakes is in twenty minutes," Harold exclaimed excitedly, grabbing the check to pay.

The friends bundled up again, walked out the door and up the stairs to the street, and started walking back to Michigan Avenue.

The gals made their stop and said goodbye to the sailors. Shirley and Clyde took a moment to embrace and kiss before leaving. It was not a casual kiss but a kiss for someone special. They knew this was something special tonight.

"Goodbye, Clyde. Write me as soon as you can. I had a wonderful time. Thank you. I'm glad you asked me out tonight," Shirley said softly in his ear.

"I'll write first thing in the morning if I can. Great time. You're wonderful. See you soon," Clyde replied. As the sailors hurried to their bus stop, they waved and said, "See you later!"

The cold sailors returned to base at 2135, just before curfew at 2200. Clyde couldn't sleep much, thinking about his wonderful time with Shirley. With a smile, he wondered what the future might hold for this relationship, this war, and this West Virginia boy. He knew he had to try to find out soon before he was shipped out to his post in the Navy.

Reveille came as usual at 0500 on Monday morning. There was little time for a sailor to sleep after an evening with a special gal. Off to chow at 0530 in the mess hall, then to the first class by 6:15. But when you think you're in love, it's even harder to concentrate on class work. Clyde and Harold were finishing their machinist classes and wrapping up their final days and exams.

The New Year's holiday was coming next weekend, and that was a perfect time for two people to enjoy the evening together, celebrating and making memories. Clyde wrote to Shirley: *28 December, 1942. Hello!*

I hope you made it home alright and didn't get too cold on the bus. We made it here by 9:35... It was best that we parted when we did because we were really tired when we got in. And we still are... The more I think about it, the more I decide not to go home this [New Year] weekend. I really can't afford it. It takes about $15 to go home [to Parkersburg, WV]. It takes $11.60 for the train and bus fare and $3 for spending. I think that's too much for such a short time, don't you?

Do you think we could make it a date then? You said I was always welcome. But this time, it will be only myself. I'm off from 4:30 Saturday [2 January] to midnight Sunday. I won't be in Chicago that long. So — do you think we could find something to do? I'll try and call you Thursday night or Friday at the latest to find out the answer, but please write soon anyway...

As always, your friend (I hope) Clyde C. McLain.

Seven - First Letters

January 1943. Shirley read her mail from Betty Hanké with excitement to get her perspective on the past weekend's date with Harold and Clyde. In those days, you wrote letters to make appointments to call a friend. No answering machines, operator-connected calls, or long-distance operators outside the city limits. A couple of dollars per call. If you needed to contact someone urgently, you would send a *Western Union* telegram hand-delivered to the address listed. Not cheap but fast. Maybe an hour or two response time. Betty wrote:

1 January 1943

Dear Shirsh,

Along with your letter, I got one from Harold...He was not happy that he didn't get a goodnight kiss like Clyde. He did say in his letter (quote), "McLain and Shirley are doing quite well — Quite well" (unquote). Is he right, or is he right? I've never seen you click with anyone so fast. From the minute you got in the car, you seemed like old friends. Maybe we'll be attending a military wedding? Remember, I'm Maid of Honor.... But seriously, Shirsh, I know how you feel. He's someone you can have fun with and keep you occupied "until the boys come home" or something...back to the Navy. You know I wouldn't let Lu [Leona Hostetter] get any ideas about Clyde. And how could I have anything to say about it? You seem to have everything under control, and how!!!!!! ...

All my love, Bets.

P.S. Say hello to HIM for me.

Friday, New Year's Day, Clyde called Shirley from the barrack's phone. "Hi, Shirley, Clyde here. How are you today? Have a good New Year's Eve?"

"Oh yeah, some of the gang for Antioch got together and had fun," Shirley replied, not wanting to get into details. "A late night, but I think I'll be rested by Sunday. What'd you think if we went down to the lake, to Soldier Field? Maybe the Aragon Ballroom? I think Dick Jurgens is playing with his band. He's a hometown boy, and this may be his last performance as a civilian before going into the Navy. The Aragon is free for men in uniform to dance. What'd you think?" Shirley hesitated for a moment for Clyde to think it over.

"Well, I guess that would be alright." Clyde was thinking about the possible cost and his delayed trip to West Virginia. "With you, anywhere is fine. Even if we just walk and talk. It would be swell just to be together for a while."

"Okay. Sunday, we'll meet at the same place in Chicago. About 2:30 like before?" Shirley suggested.

"It's a date! I can't wait to see you again. I know we'll have a swell time." Clyde and Shirley continued talking on the barracks phone for a short time until an impatient sailor told Clyde, "Hey! Time's up, hang up! It's my turn on the phone!"

Life is fluid in all ages, and plans that are made often change. Shirley couldn't get together as early as she had hoped. Family in Antioch caused her to be late and miss the train to Waukegan, and had to take the next one. They got together at about 5:30 on Sunday, 3 January. The evening was clear and not too cold, so Clyde and Shirley walked around the waterfront. They made it to the Aragon Ballroom, but it was far too noisy for conversation. So, they left, walked past Soldier Field, and eventually found a quiet place to have dinner.

"Soldier Field is scheduled to have a *War Bonds* drive next month. Some of the servicemen from the battlefield will be putting on a show. I hope we can go," Shirley said as they passed by the stadium.

"Well, Shirley, we got word today now that classes are over, we will be shipping out in the next two or three weeks. We don't know where we will be going yet, but you can be sure it's near the ocean," Clyde said in a sad and somber tone. "Our class rankings are due out this next week. Then we'll get our orders. We don't have a lot of time. I just want to keep talking and being close to you. I don't want to think about it right now."

During the war, Chicago was bustling with soldiers and sailors hanging around the waterfront, night clubs, and USO dance halls, so Clyde and Shirley were never alone.

"Let's find a place to sit and talk out of this cold night air," suggested Clyde. "Maybe there's a late-night coffee shop nearby?" And so, the evening wound down as they walked to the train station. Clyde embraced Shirley and kissed her very passionately. As Shirley boarded her train, she smiled with a tear in her eye and said, "Write me as soon as you can. It has been a very special evening. I love you, Clyde. See you soon. Bye."

"I promise to write first thing in the morning. I love you, too. Have a pleasant trip home." Clyde smiled and waved goodbye.

4 January 1943, 6:45 AM Monday

Good morning Shirley.

I promised to write first thing today, and even if I hadn't, I still would have… The train pulled out at 11:15 and arrived here at about 12:02. A little late, but all right. I was tired, and after a while, I got you off my mind… I was sleepy until I got in bed, and then I laid there thinking of you, and it was pleasant thoughts, I assure you. Tell me truthfully, were you the same way? I'm just wondering if you hated our having to part as much as I did. Please write and answer soon. I'll be looking forward to one right away. The proper way to sign this would be with "Your Friend." But somehow or other, I feel I know you better or would like to. But I am signing this,

With all my Love and Kisses, Clyde.

Like single young women of all ages, they are always looking for a fun time. However, Shirley had to decide whether to go out with Clyde or all the other friends. Another of Shirley's close friends wrote her and hoped to make plans for the next weekend, 8 January 1943. Miss June Gilmer wrote:

5 January 1943

Dear Shirley

Here I've been waiting patiently to hear from you, and I've been left at the church, so to speak. I suppose Clyde has been taking up all your spare time… love! Ah, Isn't it wonderful? [I'm] in enough trouble already. Incidentally, in case you didn't know, I was in Chicago with you kids on New Year's Eve. That is what my folks think anyway, and if you love me, don't tell them any different. I was out being a bad girl all by my lonesome that night.

What do you think about going to the Aragon this Friday night (the 8th)? The weekend after will be Dick Jurgens's last appearance as a civilian. Say, I wouldn't mind holding his sailor collar down, would you?" Do you know that Kay [Vickovich] has the measles? The three-day kind. She's broken out from head to toe. I hope she'll be able to come with us… We're all pretty broke, but that's nothing new to us. You might drop me a few lines whether I see you or not. Just make Harold, Clyde, and so on. Just wait for a day.

Sincerely June.

PS I'll try to call between 7:00 and 7:30 on Thursday night [the 6th].

Shirley had lots of mail that week. Clyde tried to explain his decision about the upcoming weekend. On Wednesday evening, Clyde wrote:

6 January 1943

Dear Shirley

I received your lovely letter today and was really glad to hear from you. I have some bad news and also some good news to tell you… First, the bad. I won't be able to see you Friday before I leave. I have decided to catch the 3:30 B&O [train] to Akron. From there, I'll go to Parkersburg… I wish I could see you this week too… I decided on this plan because it will save me some money, and I can see my relations [aunt and uncle] in Akron for a while and still have about 20 hours at home. But best of all then I can spend next weekend with you and still have all my visiting done...

If you stop to think about [train] service between Waukegan and Antioch, we would have more time together in Chicago. Anywhere is all right with me, though, because just seeing and being near you again will be like heaven, and the best way I know to spend my last liberty hours here at Great Lakes is with you. That may sound funny, but I really mean it. And don't think for one minute I'm overlooking that signature [on your letter]. How could I? It reflects my feelings, too... I've thought of you many, many times, and every time I do, I have a funny feeling go through me. I don't know how to describe it except that it is similar to the feeling you get going down a fast elevator.

Write soon... Good night,

Love and big XXX [kisses].

Clyde

12 January 1943

Dear Shirley

You aren't the only one who likes to come home and have a letter waiting for you. I got in today at 11:15 and was really glad to see your letter! Last evening with my two sisters, and I had a family picture taken... Yes, I would like to see you this weekend [16 or 17 Sunday], and the pleasure would be all mine. But it is up to you as to where. Did you mean you would stay in Chicago this weekend to please me?

You see, it cost me more for the last 160 miles by bus than it did from here to Akron, so it took my small payroll down farther than expected. I didn't spend much last time [on our date], and we had a good time, but I'm afraid I can't do as much this weekend.

I have several friends here I could borrow from, but since I won't get another payday while I'm here, I won't do it because I might be unable to pay them back...I'm not broke yet, but I won't allow a girl to pay my expenses. I don't think you can get by that easily. I'm not the kind of fellow that takes a girl out as long as she pays expenses. That's called Dutch Treat, and I'm not Dutch! So, what is it, Yes or No, and if yes, where? I'll be waiting for that answer, and I hope to get it real soon.

Love and Kisses

Clyde

17 January. Sunday morning, they met at the Chicago Union Station to travel north to Antioch, where all the fun and romance began. Clyde's only memory of that Christmas Day in Antioch was Betty, Shirley, and the snowstorm on Christmas day. The January sun shone on the glistening snow as the train lumbered northward to Shirley's family home. Meeting your best friend's parents and siblings is always a big event, particularly when you are a fresh Navy recruit from West Virginia.

Einar Petersen was there waiting to pick them up. As Shirley's big brother-in-law, he could easily toss Clyde out the window if he did not approve, or he could be Clyde's best ally. Time would tell how Einar would react to the sailor in a dark blue uniform.

The local train was on time. The windy city was calm for today. Clyde and Shirley snuggled in their seats to keep warm and be together again. "Clyde, I'm so happy that we, you, decided to meet Mom and Dad. I have talked about you until they could not take it anymore," she whispered to Clyde. "Mom is getting the family together to meet this sailor once and for all. As I have told you, we are a big family, and they can get a little rambunctious when something new is happening. So, just relax and be your regular self so they can see why I love you so much."

"I knew this time would come, and if they are as nice as you, I know I'll love them too." Clyde smiled. "Looks like we're almost at the station."

Einar greeted them at the station door. After hugging Shirley, Einar held out his hand and said, "I'm Einar Petersen, one of Shirley's four brothers-in-law."

"Clyde McLain, glad to meet you," Clyde responded with a friendly handshake. As the trio quickly walked to the car, Clyde looked around and commented, "I didn't know the town was so pretty. It was dark when I was here last time." They all laughed.

Einar drove away from the train depot and started his 'cook's tour' of the township. "Since you have never seen our pretty little town, I'll make a small detour. This is Main Street, also known as State Route 83 South. Here, you'll find almost all the businesses. Restaurants, department stores, and the Antioch Bank over there on your right. I'm turning at the bank, Lake Street, where you'll see the Antioch Theater and Ted's Sweet Shop. Ted is one of the four brothers-in-law in the family."

"Yeah, and I work there from time to time to help out. Pour sodas and help make the candy," Shirley said as she pointed to the little sweet shop.

"A short detour here on Spafford Street and to Lake Street is named for the Antioch Lake. Here on the left is Ted's house. And there on the right is where Shirley's sister Evelyn lives. Now you can see Lake Antioch." The driver turned the corner. After a few more turns, they were headed north on Hillside Avenue. "Here we are, folks, the end of the tour."

It was almost two o'clock as they entered the house and were met with delicious smells wafting from the kitchen. "Hello everyone! We're here!" Shirley announced. Clyde was a little standoffish as the crowd came to inspect the new guest. Shirley hugged all the sisters and some of the children. The menfolk were playing cards, waiting for the guest of honor to arrive.

"Mama, this is Clyde McLain," Shirley announced as Sophie came out of the kitchen wearing her flowered print apron, wiping her hands on it.

"Nice to meet you, Clyde. Make yourself at home here. With this many folks in the house, it gets a little overwhelming for a newcomer. Hope you like roast pork and spaghetti; it's Shirley's favorite." Sophie smiled and hugged Clyde. She turned to Shirley and whispered, "He's cuter than I expected for a sailor." Then, she laughed and returned to her kitchen sanctuary to finish the preparations for dinner.

Her father, C.E., was in the garage taking care of some Sunday paper accounts. He came in to find out the source of the commotion inside. "Welcome to our family, Clyde; glad to finally meet you. After all, Shirley has been telling us all about you." They shook hands, and C.E. returned to the garage to finish his work, washed up for dinner, and joined the festivities.

Einar introduced Clyde to all the brothers-in-law. First, there was Einar's brother Nels, then Edward, and lastly, Ted. They got up and shook hands. Then Shirley took Clyde into the other room, where the sisters had set up the tables. Leona, Elaine, Evelyn, and younger sister Theodora. They all had to get a hug from the good-looking sailor. What a change from the normal Naval Training Center world of smelly guys, regimentation, and rules.

"Come and get it!" shouted Sophie as she presented the roasted pork and spaghetti and placed it in the center of the dining room table. Everyone lined up in places around two tables. Eleven adults were at one table, and ten children sat at the other. Twenty-one people trying to sit down and pass food reminded Clyde of his Navy mess hall experiences.

After blessing the meal, all you could hear was the clatter of China plates and silverware with the simultaneous conversations of everyone. Parents were helping to serve the kids and men wanting to know about the war and the Naval training programs. Women talked about their food rationing problems and the latest gossip in Antioch and Chicago. Everyone had pooled their ration coupons to prepare for this memorable meal of family love and solidarity. It was the Greek way.

After an hour and a half, Shirley noticed the train back to Chicago would leave in thirty minutes. Shirley was looking for a ride to the station. "I'll drive you, folks. When do we need to leave?" volunteered Edward.

"In about ten minutes," she replied.

Ed got up and said, "I better get the car warmed now so we can leave on time."

As Clyde and Shirley said their goodbyes and put on their coats, everyone gathered to give hugs and best wishes. Clyde remarked, "I have never seen such a large family with so much love and acceptance. Your mom is something special. I never met anyone like her. She's a lot like you. Thank you for the chance to meet the family."

Arriving at the station, Edward was quiet, as always, but he remarked, "I sure am glad that you came for dinner. I pray you will return to Antioch as soon as possible and be safe in the war."

The train was right on time. Clyde sat silently, asking himself, "What just happened?" What he asked Shirley next surprised her. "What is next for us? This war is an unknown. What might happen? I would love to be with you, but I am already missing you. What is the right answer?" He went silent again, thinking about the war. Would he come home? Would he be wounded? Or never return?

"We can only know the moment. We can only love the people we are with. We cannot know the future. Only God knows the future. I wonder, too. The old saying is true: It is better to have loved and lost than to never have loved at all! I love you, Clyde! I want this war to go away so we can be normal people again," she said with a tear in her eye. "We only have tonight because you ship out in a few days. Let's enjoy this evening together. What will be, will be."

"Yes, you're right." Clyde agreed with a sigh.

"But tonight I want to DANCE! We are going to the Aragon Ballroom to dance and see the last performance of my friend Dick Jurgens. He's going to be wearing a Navy hat, just like you. And…YOU ARE COMING WITH ME! We might see Betty and Harold. Bets said they were planning to attend."

After the arrival at the Union Station, the couple had to walk a few blocks, transfer to the city 'L' line, and get off adjacent to the Aragon Ballroom. It was about 8:30 PM. The Sunday night crowd was loud and exciting. Hundreds of sailors and soldiers in uniform were in line for the next show. Service personnel in uniform got in free, and the ladies had to pay a fee. In twenty minutes, they were inside, where the noise was staggering from the bands and dancers and onlookers talking as loud as they could to be heard. With several thousand people, it was hard to find someone, anyone, that they knew. They danced to the big band sounds of Dick Jurgens' band; the Jitterbug, the Swing, and some of those slow waltzes. Clyde was not experienced in the Jitterbug, but Swing was easier to keep up with Shirley. But they both loved the slower waltz, where they could snuggle closer and maybe kiss when no one was looking.

"Clyde, let's get a couple of cocktails over at the bar. I'm exhausted?" she said while looking for a place to sit for a moment or two.

"I'll have a Gin Ricky, and the lady will have a Sloe Gin Fizz," Clyde told the bartender. "That'll be thirty-five cents for both." came the reply. Clyde found Shirley near the bar with a small round table and sat the drinks on it. "Well, I hope you enjoy this drink. I only have enough money left to get back to the base. Sip slowly." He laughed as he sat down.

They sat and laughed and held hands as they enjoyed their cocktails. "This will be a day to remember. Home-cooked food, family conversation, a beautiful sunshiny day, dancing with a beautiful gal I adore. It can't get much better than this!" He paused. "A man can leave his home and go to war remembering this moment and the reason he's fighting for a family, his girl, and a better future." And kissed Shirley once more.

"Oh no! It's quarter to eleven. I've to get going, or I'll miss my connections to the base. I'm sorry, but we have to leave," Clyde exclaimed, looking at his watch. They finished their drinks, grabbed their coats, and headed to the 'L' platform just in time for the next train.

As they rode to the final stop, Clyde said, "I'll try to call you tomorrow if the phones are working. But I promise to write you about our planned departure from the Naval Training Center."

As they got off the 'L' train they embraced for a long time, kissed, and cried for a few moments until the train had left and then walked to the street level. Shirley hailed a cab to take her to her grandmother's house in Chicago. Clyde walked a few blocks to the Great Lakes Naval Center transfer station. He was late for the midnight curfew. A night they both would remember forever.

19 January

Well, darling,

The train didn't get in until 12:20, and I got to the barracks until 12:45. But I couldn't get you off my mind long enough to sleep for a long time…

I made the rating like the fellows told me. Everyone thinks I came out with the <u>second-highest</u> average [earning a 'Second Class Petty Officer' E5 rating] of our class of 600, but there is no way to find out. I guess I'll have to take the other fellow's word for it. The top fellow in the class had an average of 93. I was about 91-92

I still know nothing about the future, but I'll call you if I can if I don't get to see you. In the meantime, keep your chin up, but don't get too many kisses from strange men? Better still, don't take any from strangers. You might get in trouble again. We know - don't we! We were strangers once.

All my love

Clyde

19 January

Hello 'Shirsh'

Guess it's my turn...Did you have a nice weekend? What did you do? How is HE?

Did you see Dick Jurgens? I saw his Sunday afternoon and evening performances. I looked around, but I don't think I could have seen you if you were there, with all the people milling around. I was almost in tears when he (Dick Jurgens) said goodbye. We got home at about 2:30 Monday morning. Did Theodora get in? Lu saw him Saturday night. How's your manicure holding out? Or did Clyde hold your hand so tight that he squeezed it all off?

Will call Thursday.

Love

Bets

When Clyde arrived in Pearl, he began writing letters to Shirley. Long letters, some twelve pages long, almost every day. The return address on the envelopes was very clear: E+R Shop, Submarine Base Pearl Harbor, T.H. (Territory of Hawaii). However, the military censors became very strict as the war dragged on. They were required to read EVERY letter from every serviceman in the area and would place a Censor Stamp on the envelope to prove it was free of any military intelligence, troop strength, locations, names of vessels, battle reports, or anything else that could give the enemy a position of strength against the U.S. Armed Forces. Eventually, Clyde was restricted to three pages per letter per day. The return address was also changed to Fleet Post Office, San Francisco, California. Clyde had to choose what to write to avoid trouble with the censor's inspections. Almost 1800 pages were written by Clyde from 1943 to 1945.

Eight - The Gang

Early 1943. "The Gang" is like an Abbot and Costello comedy *"Who's on First, and Who's on Second?"* and as complicated as a Chicago Cubs Scorecard. Clyde grew up with his mother and two sisters in Parkersburg, West Virginia. His father had left the family for work in Pittsburg, Pennsylvania, and never returned. Clyde never spoke about any childhood friends or high school buddies. His earnings as a paperboy at ten years old, in 1930, was the only cash the family had. The family raised vegetables and received "Relief" food supplements each month. As a young man without a father in the house, Clyde looked forward to being away from home. At eighteen, Clyde graduated from high school, left his sisters and mother, and went to work for his uncle on a poultry farm in Akron, Ohio. From there, he found a job as an apprentice machinist at Goodyear Rubber Company. Clyde never had a "gang" to knock around with until he met Shirley. In 1940 the 'gang' was a term of endearment for close friends.

When Clyde met Shirley, he had no idea he had become involved with two concentric circles of friends and families. Shirley and Betty had been friends since grade school, as did June, Leona, Kay, Charles, Charlie, and the Hennings families. These relationships spanned the Pacific as well as the services of the Army and Navy.

Leona and Charles Hostetter were siblings in Shirley's gang of friends. The small town of Antioch, Illinois, became the center of their world during the war. Charles Hostetter was based out of Pearl Harbor with Sid Soncek and Clyde. Clyde stepped into this web of servicemen with their girlfriends, later to become their wives. June Gilmer Soncek wrote that she had received over 100 letters from Sid and that *"between Sid and Clyde, they were keeping the Military Censors and the Post Office busy."*

The "Gang of Four Charlies" becomes very confusing: Charles Hostetter, Charlie Doerr, Charlie Gerst, and Charles Brown. Now, add to the confusion, June Gilmer dated Charlie Doerr and Sid Soncek, whom she eventually married on February 12, 1943. Charlie Doerr married Leona Hostetter, whose brother is Charlie Hostetter. Charlie Gerst was also from Illinois and worked with Clyde in the same Submarine Base Electrical and Repair machine shop at Pearl Harbor. Charlie Gerst married Kay Vickovich. Lastly, Clyde's younger sister Ellen McLain married an Atlantic sailor named Charles Brown. Ellen and Charles Brown were married in New York City on August 9, 1945. All of these people were written about in Clyde's letters to Shirley.

The girls, Shirley, Betty, Leona, June, Kay, and a few others, had great fun and sport with the soldiers and sailors in the Chicago area. The first four young women had graduated from Antioch High School in 1940. Betty and Shirley worked at several businesses in the Antioch and Chicago area, as did Leona and June.

Betty Hanké, Shirley's best friend, was on the honor roll at Antioch High School and lived all her life in Antioch.

She was a lovely young woman with a very gracious spirit and very well dressed in the "modern" fashions. Betty writes often of finding special dresses or shoes. Once, she wrote about going all out and "splurging" to buy a new hat, which cost $2.50, but she bought it for only $2.00! At that time, Betty worked at *Pickard China Company Factory*[5] as a secretary, where she got a whole 25 cents per week raise and was now making 70 cents per day! So, you can see why she was so excited to buy her hat for 50 cents off. The savings was almost a day's pay! Her mother would alter her skirts and dresses so she always looked prim and proper.

These were the "modern" women of the 1940s. June Gilmer writes, during a visit to her grandmother's house, that her *"grandmother would not go out in public with me when I was wearing my slacks."* June also wanted to take additional "business" and accounting classes. Her grandmother again rebuked her for not staying home and being a *"proper lady."* Eventually, June got it all. She worked in a large accounting office where she was taught to operate the *"IBM machine, a punch-card tabulating machine."*

As normal young women, if they liked the guy, he got their address and phone number. And what to do if you can't get rid of them? Just don't write back or return the calls. However, once or twice, the "girls" ran into one of the rejected sailors on the street. Poor *"ol' Lawrence"* found a group of Shirley's friends waiting for a bus stop in Chicago,

---

[5] *Pickard China* has been made in Antioch, Illinois, since 1893. Several US Presidents have used their hand-painted chinaware in the White House, Air Force One, including well-known hotels, and royalty.

and he followed them all night, even when they ignored him. He wrote Shirley and others a few times, but judging by his words, she did not return the favor. But after that experience, Shirley's friends' letters were full of laughter at Lawrence's expense. Once, Betty wrote to Shirley: *"Better go lightly on the red paint [lipstick], it's getting hard to come by."* (i.e., Lipstick supplies were limited due to rationing during the war years.) *"So many sailors and so little time, what's a girl to do?"*

These gals were like single gals of any age and were always thinking of the guys they had met or might meet. Their letters are replete with chatter about the men they met at the dances or on the buses or trains. The Aragon Ballroom was a legendary meeting place and dancehall. The Aragon Ballroom, built in 1926, covered an entire city block. With the Chicago 'L' (elevated train) serving its front door, the Aragon could easily accommodate 18,000 patrons in a six-day week. Built-in the Moorish architectural style to resemble a small Spanish village, complete with the nighttime skies projected upon its large arched ceiling for all the happy patrons to enjoy. Its gigantic dance floor was surrounded by arched colonnades containing meeting rooms, food service, and bars, with a large stage for the band to serenade the dancers. One gal wrote a postcard to Shirley in February 1943, *"We're here tonight having a gay time. More sailors here than are in the Navy. I have worn out a pair of shoes already. Love Carol."*

Shirley had letters from many people, both men, and women. Most men were in the service and were hometown friends or family members. Army Air Force Sergeant Frank J. Cali Jr. wrote several times in 1942 until March 1943, when he found out about Clyde. Sergeant Cali went on to Laredo, Texas, to teach *"flexible gunnery"* to bomber crews and most likely went on to the European theaters as a gunner on a B-17 bomber.

Charlie Doerr, an old Antioch High School friend, was a Private First Class (PFC) in the Army Artillery Corps. He dated June Gilmer until he went to the Army. Charlie joined, or was drafted into, the Army about July 1941, before the war. After the war was declared, his Army squad set up anti-aircraft guns on the roof of an airplane factory in Southern California. Later, he was in the Aleutian Islands during the Japanese conquest of two Aleutian Islands, Attu, and Kiska, in June 1942. As an artillery gunner, Charlie most likely shelled the Japanese fortifications during the American campaign to retake those two islands and to rebuild Dutch Harbor, which had been bombed by the Japanese in 1942. Charlie was still in Alaska during Christmas 1943 and sent *"Christmas Greetings"* to Shirley. The Aleutian Islands Campaign lasted until 15 August 1943 and was as difficult and costly as any island battle in the South Pacific. It has been called the *"forgotten battle in the Pacific."* Charlie went on to marry his old friend Leona Hostetter and moved back to Antioch for a short time after the war. The Doerr's and McLain's were westward bound in 1948.

June Gilmer wrote to Charlie Doerr while in the Army but enjoyed her nights out with the girls. One day in late fall 1942, she met Sid Soncek, a sailor at Great Lakes Training Center – where all the new recruits are sent – and quickly found herself in the middle of two guys talking marriage, one at hand and one in Alaska. June wrote about this dilemma to Shirley at Christmas 1942. The problem quickly worked itself out because, by 6 February, 1943, June wrote to Shirley that *"all the gang is fine and dandy"* in Antioch. *"I'm really riding the clouds"* as she announced her plans to marry Sid the following week, 12 February. They were married in New York City and honeymooned in Boston because Sid, a torpedo man (TM2/c), and had been assigned to the new USS Lexington (CV16) aircraft carrier, which was being prepared to set sail from New York harbor to the Pacific theater.

Charles Gerst went into the Navy before Clyde and was already working at the Submarine Base Repair shop when Clyde arrived. Clyde and Charles met via the *"gang from Antioch,"* and the two sailors spent much of their liberty together, usually talking about Shirley and Kay. Charles and Kay were married while on stateside leave in the summer of 1944. Charles later became frustrated with his base duties and volunteered for submarine duty. In October 1944, Charles was assigned to the USS Kingfish (SS-234) as a Torpedo-man First Class (TM1/c). While Charles was assigned to the Kingfish submarine, he participated in Ninth through the Twelfth War Patrols and saw combat service off the coast of Japan. By August 1945, Charles was transferred to Mare Island Naval Base in California, where he and Kay set up housekeeping with their new daughter.

Nine - In The Navy Now

22 January 1943. As with many military activities, plans are meant to be changed without notice. The old axiom is true in the Navy, too: "Hurry up and wait." The planned Wednesday troop train departure was pushed back to Friday at 0245. Clyde was writing his lament over loss of sleep and waiting at the train station on the base, loaded and standing waiting for two days. The 22 January letter gave his new address as Treasure Island Naval Base, San Francisco, California.

By Sunday, the train full of servicemen had passed through Kansas, Colorado, and New Mexico. For a West Virginia boy who lived on the Ohio River, the mountains in Colorado were an incredible sight. The Painted Desert bluffs of New Mexico were works of art. The snow line was high above the city. Clyde's letter posted from Gallup, New Mexico, on 24 January was written on USO (United Service Organization) letterhead stationery and was notated: "Idle Gossip Sinks Ships." The train lumbered over the Continental Divide across Arizona and the Sierra Nevada mountains and north through California's central valley. The train arrived in Oakland, where the servicemen were dispersed to their various bases around the Bay Area. [6]

Clyde and Harold, and the other sailors from Great Lakes were taken by a large ferryboat to Treasure Island Naval Base in the middle of the San Francisco Bay. Clyde had lots of freedom to move around the base and Bay Area until he was assigned to a ship. To add insult to injury, he was flat broke with no paycheck possible until he was aboard his assigned ship. His letter was signed off "Treasure Island, San Francisco, CA" on 27 January. [7]

On 21 January 1943, one of Pan-American Airline's famous Philippine Clipper airplanes, a seaplane or flying boat, struck a mountain near San Francisco on approach to

---

[6] History records that as many as 114,000 special troop trains were used during World War II. Ogden, Utah's Union Station boasted 120 trains per day traveling through its tracks.

[7] Treasure Island was originally built for the Golden Gate International Exposition (World's Fair) of 1939-1940, with several 1930s Art Deco exposition halls. In preparation for the fair, the San Francisco-Oakland Bay Bridge was built in 1935-1936, and the Golden Gate Bridge was built in 1936-1937. The 3 to 4-square-mile island was constructed in 1936-1937 by placing rocks in the water and piling up material to create a land mass. After the Exposition closed in 1940, Pan American Airlines took over the island as an airport for their famous "China Clipper" flying boats. The PanAm Clippers were the first true transcontinental airplanes serving Honolulu, Manila, and China. In September 1942, the Navy took over the airbase island, where military-style barracks were built, and contracted PanAm to do submarine watch off the Pacific coast. Later, the hangar buildings were converted to barracks for US Naval personnel in transit to the Pacific theaters. Most of the sailors shipping out were housed on Treasure Island until their deployment. Over two million men were housed temporarily at the base. At the peak of the war, 12,000 men per day were processed for their duty stations at Treasure Island. The Naval base closed in 1993.

the Treasure Island airfield, and all aboard perished. Needless to say, the talk on Treasure Island must have been heavy about that recent crash when Clyde arrived on 27 January.

In his letter of 29 January, Clyde said that Harold had called Betty Hanké, and Clyde said "Hello" too. Clyde told Shirley he was concerned about ever seeing her again because of the great uncertainty of the war, and she was free to do as she wished. 3 February, the sailors were notified that they would ship out on Friday, 5 February. As always, the US Navy told the men they were being assigned to the Pacific Fleet Command. That was all they knew. The exact ship or station would be announced in Pearl Harbor. Just pack your gear and get ready to board the Military Sea Transport Ship (MSTS) waiting at Mare Island, Vallejo, CA, about 20 miles north of Treasure Island. That was all they knew.

Clyde's words were very distressed as he broke the news to Shirley. He talked about dreaming of coming back to Illinois and marrying the love of his life. He said he would make a "formal" proposal when he could do it in person with a ring. But he was concerned that he may be injured or killed in the war. However, he was anxious to "get to work" and end the war. [8]

Still with his feet firmly on land, on February 5, Clyde says the first transfer of sailors to the ship would be

---

[8] The two great naval battles of Midway Island in June 1942 and of Guadalcanal in November 1942 must have weighed heavily on the minds of these young sailors preparing for war. In these two battles alone, the US Navy had lost over 2000 men, and at least 11 ships were sunk.

Sunday the 7th. The MSTS ship was loaded with thousands of sailors and troops for the trip to Hawaii, which would normally take seven to ten days. On 22 February, he wrote that he had been in Pearl Harbor for a few days and was settling in but had not yet received his final assignment. Clyde commented about Hawaii's beauty and mild climate and that he would like to live there after the war, which was somewhat prophetic.

Stateside mail had begun to arrive, and Shirley's Valentine's Day card was a big hit when it arrived. Clyde sent her a photo of himself in his white sailor's uniform, which was the standard dress code for the Pacific Fleet sailors.

Each day, ships and submarines were returning to Pearl Harbor in need of repair from the battles, and as a Machinist Mate 2nd Class (MM2/c), Clyde had to have been in high demand. He was assigned to the Electrical and Repair Machine Shop 1 in the Submarine Base in Pearl Harbor, an assignment that could last a few months or years. Harold also made the trans-Pacific journey and was assigned to the same machine shop as Clyde. They had to repair machinery of all types and manufacture the replacement parts when none existed.

Navy life was completely different from Boot Camp or anything else Clyde had experienced. Seeing the horrors of the Pearl Harbor attack on December 7, 1941, for the first time was chilling, angering, and sobering. Clyde and Harold *"manned the rails"* in their US Navy blue uniforms as the MSTS ship entered Pearl Harbor Naval Base at 0700 hours. As they stood at attention, they could not believe the carnage and destruction stretched out before them. Battleships to the left and other ships in various stages of collapse. Blacked steel skeletons of fighting ships lying on their sides. The battleships Oklahoma, West Virginia, Utah, and others were visible as the sailors entered the harbor. Workers were busy cutting up the steel carcasses to salvage anything of value for repairs. [9] [10]

---

[9] The USS Arizona was sunk early in the attack on December 7. She took several direct hits from the torpedoes the attacking Japanese airplanes dropped. The explosions were so great that the ship sank almost immediately to the bottom of the harbor. One thousand one hundred seventy-seven sailors are still entombed in its iron hull, which is today a US National Memorial site. Parts of a big gun turret and a silhouette of the deck are still visible from the Memorial platform built in 1962. Oil droplets, called the "Tears of Arizona," still rise to the surface each day as an eerie reminder of the destruction and loss of life from that terrible day in December 1941. The battleship, USS Missouri, on which the Japanese surrender of 1945 was signed, now floats at rest near the Arizona Memorial. The Missouri, or "Mighty Mo" as she was called, ended the WWII conflict that had begun with the sinking of the Arizona. In 1999, she was decommissioned and moved to Pearl Harbor. One of the last trips that Clyde would ever take was to walk the decks and climb the ladders of that huge battleship in 2006, and had a view of the Sub Base Rescue Tower for the last time, which made such an indelible mark on his life. He was once again a 23-year-old sailor in his heart.

[10] The battleship West Virginia was sunk on December 7, 1941, and lay in shallow water at its pier. Seven Japanese torpedoes had entered the hull and rolled on its side. It was raised and put into a dry dock in Pearl Harbor until May 7, 1943, when it sailed for the Seattle, Washington, area. It returned to the WWII battle in October 1943. However, the battleship Oklahoma was so badly damaged that it would never fight again. It was fully capsized, and righting and re-floating the huge ship began in late 1942. By November 1943, it was floating and towed to the dry dock for salvage operations. The damage was so great that the guns, machinery, and ammunition were removed, and she lay at anchor in Pearl Harbor until 1946, when she was sold as scrap. The USS Utah quickly rolled over and sank; 58 men were killed, but the vast majority of her crew could escape. The wreck remains in Pearl Harbor, and in 1972, a memorial was erected near the ship.

"Harold, can you believe this? How could anyone survive this battle?" Clyde said under his breath, in respect for the fallen servicemen. "It makes me cry just thinking about those poor guys in the Arizona and other ships. It makes your blood boil in anger. It's worse than the newsreels and radio described it. It's been fifteen months, and they are still trying to remove the damaged ships."

Harold just shook his head in agreement. He said, "It's a sight I'll never forget."

The PA speaker announced, "All passengers, prepare to disembark from the Promenade Deck in fifteen minutes."

It was a sea of blue and olive drab uniforms waiting to walk down the gangways toward dry land. Busses were organized for the different GI units, Marines, Navy, and a few Army soldiers. The Navy barracks were about the same as Treasure Island or Mare Island, California, but it was very hot and nearly one hundred percent humidity. It was easy to tell the new recruits from the seasoned sailors. The heat and humidity were unbearable in the Navy-blue wool uniforms of the recruits. Just a month ago, these guys were in Chicago's winter storms. But in Pearl, white cotton uniforms were the uniform of the day, or light blue dungarees for working.

The buses let their passengers off at the supply terminal to collect their new whites, dungarees, and other items for their sea bags. As each sailor received his gear, he was directed to his barrack assignment. Once settled at the barracks, it was time to walk to the chow hall for lunch.

"Hey Clyde, I can't wait to change out of these blues. I can hardly breathe. But it's nice touching terra firma again. Are you having trouble walking again?"

"Ah, me too. I think they say, 'you have to get your Land-legs back' because you've been on the ship so long you've grown Sea-legs." Clyde laughed as he swaggered with every step. Back to the barracks and organize their insignia and rating patches to be sewn on the new white uniforms. Clyde put on his new stripes of a Machinist Mate, Second Class Petty Officer (MM2/c), for the first time.

Standard Navy time: Reveille, 0500, Chow, 0600, Formation Inspection Roll Call, 0700. After the roll call, the assignments were made, and buses were waiting. Harold and Clyde boarded their assigned Navy gray bus, and it lumbered down toward the various docks and shipyards on the base. Sailors got off at aircraft carriers, destroyers, cruisers, submarines, and some dry docks. Clyde and Harold were the last two sailors on the bus.

"Hey, what about us?" Clyde asked the driver

"It says here, McLain and Jensen, go to the Submarine Repair Shop Number 1. Is that you boys?" The driver reads his list. "The Sub Repair shop is around the other side of these piers and docks. Subs come in for repairs on the next pier. We'll be there in a few minutes."

"Well, Harold, I guess we're getting the Cook's Tour around the base." Clyde laughed.

The driver pulled up in front of the Submarine Repair Shop. "Here you guys are. Better look lively; this is a very busy shop."

As Clyde and Harold grabbed their stuff and got off the bus, the Chief Petty Officer in charge of the Repair Shop walked out. "You the recruits? It's about damn time you showed up. We've been short-handed for months. Get inside and talk to the Petty Officer in the back about your lockers, tools and assignments. This shop runs all day and night. We have five or six boats docked and waiting for upgrades. Meet me in the office in twenty minutes. Got projects for you two."

A few weeks later, in the Chief's office, "Clyde, we just got several new RADAR setups for the subs. Take a couple of guys who are not busy and get the measurements for the installations on the boat docked outside. They need their RADAR installed before they can shove off." The Chief ordered. "I have another crew installing the sea-mine protection frames there now."

Radio Detection And Ranging (RADAR) was in limited use in 1939 by the British. They shared the technology with the USA and a few Commonwealth Countries during the early days of World War II. Adaptions for submarine use came in 1942-43 and made a huge contribution to the war effort. The water-tight steel shipping boxes containing RADAR parts were slowly arriving in Pearl. One of those boxes would later be used to send Clyde's tools and belongings back to Mare Island in October 1945.

Clyde and two other machinists hustled over to the docks. Every submarine is a little different in measurements, so the team had to take all of the measurements and compare them to the installation standards. Placement of the antennas, cable openings, mounting, and power locations. Afterward, the team began cutting and welding the various parts for installation. Most of the older boats were retrofitted with RADAR when they returned to Pearl Harbor for refueling and repairs in between patrols.

RADAR was used to locate surface ships and airplanes. The major problem with the early electronic system was that it could not determine who was an enemy or a friend. Larger ships, multiple ships, or planes would show up in the large round display as a dot on the screen. The operator could determine distance and speed by calibrated tables, but all sightings were treated as 'enemies' until radio identification could be confirmed via radio codes.

Two hundred sixty-three submarines were used in World War II, and they all needed this new technology as soon as possible. A friendly fire damaged or sunk several submarines because of radio 'blackout' orders. This system allowed the sub-commander to plan an attack and locate all potential attackers. The new RADAR systems were second priority after repairs from battle damage to ensure the submarine's seaworthiness.

A few weeks later, Clyde got a special request. Most of the sailors called Clyde 'Mac,' which is short for Machinist Mate. Short nicknames for higher ranked enlisted men with specialty fields were common onboard ships and on base. Currently Clyde the lead machinist in the shop.

"Mac!" Yelled the Chief. "The Lieutenant wants you to talk to the Captain of the sub that docked earlier this week. He needs a good machinist for some reason. A special G-job (personal job) for the captain."

"Right away, Chief." Mac grabbed his hat and a clipboard and was dock-side in a few minutes.

"Permission to come aboard?" Mac saluted the Officer of the Deck (OD) and the American Flag on the stern.

"What can I do for a sailor?" the OD asked.

"I have a special request from the Captain," Mac replied.

"I'll let him know you're here." The OD picked up the ship's phone.

"Captain says he'll meet you at his wardroom. I'll get a guide for you." The OD waved to one of the crewmen standing nearby.

After proper salutes and introductions, the Captain said, "I have a very special request for you. Heard you were the best machinist in the shop. As you may have heard, we were in a firefight and took a direct hit. But by the grace of God, the shell was a dud. It only penetrated the outer shell and not the pressure hull. Otherwise, we could have been sent to Davy Jones' Locker. Instead, we made port for repairs." Captain paused.

" Yes, Sir Captain. How can I help?" Clyde inquired.

The Captain turned and grabbed hold of a large, five-inch US Navy shell, all scratched and discolored. "This shell was taken out of the side of this sub. It's been defused and is only an empty piece of US Navy ordnance." He handed it to Mac. "We had to maintain radio silence, and one of our destroyers thought we were a Japanese sub and started firing at us. We used the signal lights and Morse Code to signal them to stop shooting at us. Their poor marksmanship and this dud is the only reason we are still afloat. I want you to make a trophy out of it for me. People will never believe my story until I show them this shell."

"Yes, Sir. How soon do you get underway, Sir?" Clyde quickly imagined what he could make.

"Our next patrol starts in three weeks or as soon as all updates and the RADAR are complete."

"Surprise me with something to keep people talking. Name and date stuff. Okay?"

"Sir, I'll get right on it. Be in touch, Sir." Clyde saluted, turned, exited the wardroom, and returned to the Repair Shop.

"Hey Mac, what's that you got? Looks like a 5-inch shell. Is one of the destroyers giving them away?" One of the shop machinists laughed and looked the shell over.

"The sub-captain wants a trophy made out of this dud shell." Clyde shook his head and laughed at the story behind the shell.

"If I can find a 5-inch casing, I can cut the base, refit the shell, and make a place for writing. Anything else could take a lot of thought." Clyde wondered. "Maybe just a base to stand upright and show off the mangled shell tip. Date and ship number, Captain's name on a faceplate."

By the end of 1943, all submarines had the SJ version of the Radar system installed, and it increased the accuracy and safety of the sub patrols. And it may have helped reduce any 'friendly fire.'

Ten - Torpedoes

31 August 1943. Submarine Captains had been complaining about non-exploding torpedoes for months. They would hit their targets, verified by the sound of the steel-on-steel contact, but the torpedo did not explode, i.e., a dud. Admiral Charles Lockwood, Commander of the Pacific Submarine Fleet, took charge of the problems. Lockwood appointed Admiral Charles Momsen, Commander of the Submarine Squadron 2, to conduct the tests to determine the problems. Several submarine Captains were in Pearl Harbor and assisted Momsen and Lockwood in solving these issues: First detonation failures, Second depth readings incorrect, and Third torpedo circular runs.

The Submarine Repair Shop Chief called out to Clyde, "Lieutenant just ordered us to get over to the Rescue Tower on the double. The Admiral is pullin' out all the stops. They're right in the middle of a great Congressional investigation regarding these damned torpedoes that won't explode. They need the best machinist right now! Which is you, McLain!"

"Sure Chief. This stuff can wait. What can I do for you?" Clyde replied.

"You come with me." The Chief motioned to Clyde and started to walk off. Clyde followed.

"Alright, Clyde, they're working on a huge problem with our Mark 14 torpedoes that are used in subs, patrol boats, and aircraft. Only about ten percent of those fish explode on impact. The sub-captains are raising hell with Admiral Mumsen. And he's got the Bureau of Ordnance and Congressmen crawling all over this base. And you've just stepped into a hornet's nest. We're headed to the Submarine Rescue Training Tower. You can't miss it. It's a hundred feet high, the tallest thing on the base. They have it set up to drop some fish, ah torpedoes, on a steel plate to see why them firing pins aren't firing."

The Rescue Tower was a couple hundred yards away. As they arrived, one torpedo was dropped from about fifty feet. The steel fish hit the steel target plate with the sound of a 5-inch gun. Kaboom!

All the important Naval Brass were present, and the Bureau of Ordnance engineers were attempting to dissect the torpedo and retrieve the firing pin assembly. The Sub Repair Shop Lieutenant discussed what they thought was wrong with the engineers.

"Chief, the unit has to be disassembled carefully, and measurements need to be taken to determine the cause of failure." Lieutenant said. "We have to get on this with all haste, top priority, understand? I'll check on your progress in an hour or so."

"Yes Sir, we'll get right on it. Our new top-rated machinist just arrived. The engineers gave us the spec drawings. Anything else, Sir?" The Chief saluted and was dismissed.

"There's a lot of lives waiting for this fix," the Chief said. "These torpedoes have three major problems. First, they run twenty feet deeper than their depth indicator setting and slide under the hulls of almost every ship. Second, the gyroscope that keeps them running straight fails, and the fish circles back to sub, and we sunk a few of our subs. And third, the detonators are magnetic and jam, break, or bend but don't trigger an explosion. And if that happens, the trail of air bubbles can be spotted by the enemy and reveal the sub's position. Up to eighty percent failure rate."

"Wow, what do you want me to do?" Clyde asked as the two hustled back to the Repair Shop.

"Measure the various components, both good and bad, to see what has bent or smashed or misshaped compared to the specs. And get some ideas of what went wrong. The shop has all the tools you need, and some of the fellas may have some experience with these torpedoes," Chief said. "This is a big one, and everyone is looking at us."[11]

---

[11] The WWII Mark 14 torpedoes were designed in the late 1930s and really never had a wartime test. The Mark 14 torpedo was designed to run by steam propulsion. Grain alcohol was used with compressed air to create steam for the small turbine engine on each torpedo. The Mark 14 was plagued with three major design flaws: the firing pins and the guidance systems, which were all mechanical. The third problem was with the steam-driven Mark 14 torpedoes. When on a "run" to the target, the exhaust left a trail of steam air bubbles in the water that could be seen by enemy surface ships and aircraft and locate the submarine. The Mark 6 detonator had a faulty design, and the entire cash of torpedoes had to be reworked with the new design developed in the sub-repair shop where Clyde worked. Clyde wrote in his memoirs that he was the one who made the first working prototype solution for the Mark 6 detonator.

At the shop, Clyde and the Chief opened the torpedo detonator on the bench. The clockwork mechanism was spread over the workbench, including the firing pin, ratchet wheels, pawls, gears, and bearings. "The torpedo men set these gears for distance to the target. As the torpedo, powered by compressed air and an alcohol motor, travels, the gears wind down and arm the detonator. Once armed, the magnetic firing pin would trigger the explosion," Chief explained as he pointed out the parts of the detonator.

"See here, how this firing pin is bent? The whole frame is bent. Too tight for it to move." Chief noticed. "The magnets are causing the pin to bind on the steel frame. Needs a non-magnetic pin."

"We can remake the housing and pins out of aluminum stock," one of the torpedo men suggested. "We have a huge stock of salvaged aluminum. We recovered several Japanese planes and saved the aluminum for use in the shop. It would be great to send some of those Japanese planes back to Tokyo in a torpedo!" The whole crew laughed. "Yeah, it sure would!"

The repairmen retrieved the aluminum stock and recast it into blocks for the milling machines and lathes. After many trials and errors, a new design was ready for testing. The prototype detonator was loaded and dropped from the tower as before. Second, third, and more test prototypes were made until they all worked successfully.

The Mark 14 torpedoes were almost the worst enemy we had at the start of WWII. Some have suggested that if the torpedo problems had not existed at the beginning of the Pacific Campaign, the war with Japan could have been over in late 1944. A year earlier.

30 September 1943. With the prototypes approved, the Sub Base machinists began manufacturing a full complement of new parts for real torpedoes. The USS Barb (SS-220) was the first sub-loaded with the new torpedoes and put to sea. The new firing pins were then installed on all available submarines for testing in actual wartime combat.

The Bowfin (SS-287) and other participating subs began testing the new torpedoes when they were available in late summer of 1943. The new design was sent to other submarine repair shops throughout the Pacific Theater. Rework continued until new versions were available from the Bureau of Ordnance, which took until late 1944, almost a year later. A strange irony of the war with Japan is that the Japanese planes that bombed Pearl Harbor on December 7, 1941, that had been shot down, were now being used to sink Japanese ships and bring an end to the war![12]

---

[12] The Shinano, a 68059-ton aircraft carrier, was converted from a battleship while under construction at Yokosuka, Japan. She was the largest aircraft carrier built prior to the late 1950s. Partially completed on 9 November 1944, the Shinano was sent from the Yokosuka Naval Arsenal to Kure Naval Base to complete outfitting and load 50 Yokosuka MXY7 Ohka rocket-propelled kamikaze flying bombs. En route to Kure, she was sunk on 19 November 1944, 10 days after commissioning, by four torpedoes from the American submarine USS Archer-Fish (SS-311). The Shinano carried an inexperienced crew, had serious design and construction flaws, and was not ready for combat. Over a thousand of her crew and passengers were rescued, but 1,435 sailors and civilians died, including her Captain. Shinano remains the largest warship ever sunk by a submarine.

The Wahoo (SS-238) [13] Had experienced a full complement of duds (2 of 20 exploded), and her Captain pressed the issue with Admiral Lockwood. Earlier, the Wahoo had returned from her fourth patrol with the 'Clean Sweep' broom on its periscope. She entered Pearl from her fourth patrol, demonstrating the crew's ability to sink ships. Frustrated with the Mark 14 torpedoes, she loaded up a test of the new replacement Mark 18 torpedoes and left Pearl on 9 September.

The Tang (SS-306), also exasperated with the Mark 14 troubles, loaded the new Mark 18s to test them in battle. The Tang has been credited with sinking 33 vessels, which was itself sunk by its new Mark18 torpedo. On its final patrol attack, 24 October 1944, the torpedo made a circular run and hit the stern of the submarine. As the boat, which was on the surface, slowly slipped below the waves, five sailors in the conning tower were blown overboard. Thirteen escaped from the forward section using the 'Momsen Lung' (designed by Admiral Momsen, who was trying to solve the torpedo problems), but only eight made it to the surface alive. Only nine souls, including Commander Richard

---

[13] The Wahoo was one of the most decorated submarines, with twenty enemy kills. She left Pearl Harbor on 9 September to begin her seventh patrol in the Sea of Japan. She never returned, sunk by the Japanese planes on 9 October 1943. In October 2006, the Wahoo was located, and the US Navy conducted an Eternal Patrol Service.

O'Kane, were 'rescued' by the Japanese ships that they had been targeting and were sent to prison camps in Japan.[1415]

Before long, the Repair Shop was back refitting torpedoes for the fleet. Some 30,000 torpedoes in the Pacific had to be refitted. RADAR and other upgrades were needed for all the Pacific Fleet subs.

---

[14] The Japanese surrender on 2 September 1945 allowed the Allied forces to empty the prisoner-of-war camps in Japan and elsewhere. Commander Richard O'Kane and the remaining crew were repatriated and returned to the USA. In March 1946, President Harry Truman awarded the Congressional Medal of Honor to Commander O'Kane. His Naval career continued, and he retired as Rear Admiral. Commander O'Kane had been the Executive Officer of the Wahoo on its first six patrols and was transferred to the Tang as Commanding Officer and provided details of Tang's final days.

[15] The wreckage of SS Tang was found in the Formosa Strait in the early 1950s by a US destroyer.

Eleven - Torpedo Juice

Whenever men are left to their own devices with free time, somebody starts looking for alcohol to relax and loosen up from the stresses of war. The Naval personnel in Pearl Harbor were no different. The fact was that there were only a few bars or pubs to imbibe. Most of the civilian bars in Honolulu were off-limits to the GIs. With only a few military beer gardens on the bases. So, where could a really thirsty GI go to get a real cocktail? Nowhere! So, why not build a still? But where would the grain come from to distill the liquor? Torpedoes, naturally! Who would have ever thought that your friendly Navy sub base was the closest liquor dispensary? Good old Yankee ingenuity at its best!

Torpedo Juice, as it became known, was one of those wartime stories of which legends and myths are made. First, it was a cocktail drink, then a book, and lots of other nostalgia-like things. Clyde writes about this in his memoirs below. The following story sounds more like an episode of TV's McHale's Navy than a wartime story.

Clyde had been working the midnight shift for six months. Twelve-hour shifts seven days a week. As he entered the Repair Shop, he smelled something strange. Not oil or diesel or welding slag.

"Hey, what's the strange smell?" he asked the new machinist, TorpedoMan (T/M3c).

"Didn't think you would notice," the machinist replied. "Some of the guys made a small still for making alcohol. The old alcohol from the torpedoes is distilled into moonshine. They call it Torpedo Juice. The Chief and Lieutenant are gone for a few days. So, we fired it up. Do you want a taste? We mix it with pineapple juice. Not too bad!"

"Well, not now, maybe later. And besides, I heard that stuff can kill you or make you blind. On second thought, I think I'll pass." Clyde shook his head in disbelief as he walked away.

A few days later, the Chief returned and found the still. He raised hell with the Torpedo Juice Gang (TJG). Told them to get rid of it before the Lieutenant returned. So, as good, resourceful sailors, not wanting to waste liquor, they poured the batch into an old coffee pot. The still was hidden, and the sailors kept nursing the old coffee pot until the Chief poured a cup.

"What the hell! I told you, boys, get this liquor out of here!" the Chief yelled.

"Chief, got a moment? Got a few things to take care of for the Commander," the Lieutenant said as he entered the Repair Shop. He walked up and started to pour a cup of coffee from the same pot.

"Sir! The coffee in this other pot is fresher. I'll get you a cup!" the Chief responded quickly, but it was too late. The 'hi-test coffee' was at the Lieutenant's lips.

"What the hell!? Who made this coffee? Best stuff I've tasted in Pearl!" he said with a big grin. "But if you 'swabbies' don't want to be hangin' over the side of some ship chipping paint for the rest of this war, you're going to stop making moonshine and start fixing them damned torpedoes! Chief, in your office. Now!"

The crew quickly got back to work and listened to the Chief get reamed out. Later that day, the Torpedo Juice Gang removed the old batch of liquor and moved the still to a place in the back under a workbench. Thinking that was the end of the problem, the crew left the area and started work on other projects.

At midnight, Second Class Petty Officer Clyde, 'Mac' as he was called, and his crew relieved the day shift. However, the TJG forgot to turn off the still when they left. At about 0300, the still exploded, and all the dock workers came running to investigate. Surprisingly, no fire ignited, but the shop was a mess of water, steam, and broken pipes. As night shift supervisor, Clyde instructed the crew, "Clean up this mess and remove all evidence of the still before you do anything else. If the Chief or Lieutenant finds out, we'll all get busted to Seaman Apprentice again."

Scuttlebutt in the Navy is always listening. When the day shift crew arrived, the Chief was with them. They had already heard about the still explosion. The Chief called, "All hands fall in for muster in the shop." As the two crews came to attention, the Chief continued, "I'm going to conduct a thorough investigation. You better fess up, now, who's at fault, because if I find the still or any of its parts, the whole shop will be on report. And God help you if the Lieutenant finds out before I do!"

"Mac, give me the full story. I want names," Chief bellowed with a frown on his face.

"Chief, I can assure you that my crew made a thorough inspection after the incident, and all offending materials have been removed from the shop," came Mac's reply.

"Give me some names. Who's been cooking this stuff?"

"Not my night crew, Chief, must have been the day shift. We have too many torpedoes to work on, and the RADAR installations had half of the guys on board the subs all night."

"This is your last warning. Dismissed!" The Chief walked to his office. The Chief reassured the Lieutenant that he had dealt with the still issue and got back to work.

The next morning at muster, with both day and night crews of sub-engineers present, the Lieutenant made a point to comment on the recent alcohol still explosion. "You know, I thought you boys were top-notch engineers; yes, Sir, I did. But after that dumb-ass still stunt, I ought to send you all to the motor pool. Any engineer who doesn't know that the first thing you do is install a pressure relief valve on a boiler to keep it from exploding, is not fit to be called an engineer. Do you know that you have made me the laughingstock of the Navy? You dead-head swabbies are nothing but goof-offs. The next time, you'll be busted to Seaman Apprentice and transferred to KP for the rest of the war. Do you hear me?"

"Sir, Yes Sir!" rang out in unison. "Dismissed," came the reply.

Almost every branch of the service had Torpedo Juice under a secret workbench. There must have been a lot of thirsty sailors and soldiers after the demise of the Mark 14 torpedoes. The Mark 14 torpedo was designed to run on steam propulsion. Grain alcohol (Ethanol) was used with compressed air to create steam for the small turbine engine on each torpedo. The thirsty seamen quickly learned how to distill the alcohol and mix three parts of pineapple juice with two parts of alcohol. The 180-proof 'white lightning' would *"kick like a mule."*

The Naval authorities got wind of this underground activity and added a poisonous ingredient, methanol, to the propellant to render the alcohol undrinkable. At first, a little pink dye was added to make the poison visible and stop the men from drinking it. The methanol could cause blindness and possible death. Later, the methanol was replaced with Croton oil, which was not deadly but would empty the poor sailor's bowels almost immediately and leave a severe hangover.

The underground bootleggers found several ways to remove the poison and oil, but nothing was completely foolproof. The sailors filtered the alcohol steam through a compressed loaf of bread, which worked fairly well, and condensed into the 180-proof liquid.

In the tropics and seaside marinas you can still order a pink Torpedo Juice cocktail as a remanent for the Pacific war.

Twelve - Navy Leave Time

Charles Hostetter from Antioch, Illinois, had been working in the other Submarine Repair Shop #2 when Clyde arrived in Pearl. Occasionally, the two friends got a shift together.

"Charlie, hurry up. Got to be at Chow in five minutes. I want to get a seat and some dessert before all those new boots get in line. God knows they'll eat us out of everything."

As the two sailors started walking to the mess hall from the Submarine Repair Shop #1, Clyde continued, "Looks like we are going to have to pull some extra shifts. Several subs came in today that'll need RADAR installations."

"Yeah." Charlie sighed. "We're already backed up with the torpedo upgrades and all the big brass and government engineers from the Bureau of Ordnance hangin' around."

Clyde read the daily menu, "We're in luck; they're serving some kind of meat tonight. They call it *SPAM*. Oh well, mystery meat is still better than C-rations. Let them recruits learn how to open a tin can for once." They both laughed and got into the chow line.

After dinner, on their way back to the barracks, Charlie inquired. "Hey, Clyde. Do you want to stop by the gunny's locker and see if we can have a taste of that new batch of Torpedo Juice? They said it may be done by tonight."

"No, I'm going to do my letter writing before I hit the sack. And besides, the Lieutenant is going to be on the lookout for that still. He almost found it last month." Clyde laughed.

Charlie shook his head and smiled. "Yeah, it damned near blew up again during the morning muster call. He knew something was cookin' but didn't have time to find it before them yokels moved the still."

"And besides, I'm a beer man. Heard they got some *Pabst Blue Ribbon* at the canteen." Clyde remembered. "I'll just grab a bottle there on the way back to the barracks."

"Okay, Clyde, be that way. Just don't tell Shirl everything. I don't want the folks finding out I've been hitting the Juice. They're funny that way," Charlie said as a caution.

"Okay. I got the graveyard shift tonight, so it'll be a short night. See you next week. Maybe we can hit Honolulu in the daytime." Clyde thought, hopefully.

"Sure, that'd be swell. Gotta shove off." Charlie waved and headed off for the Sub Base Repair shop.

With twelve-hour shifts and no weekend off, a sailor might take a few hours to relax and unwind before bed or work. Writing letters home and reading correspondence from mail-call were frequent activities for the few hours left over.

5 March 1943, Clyde wrote Shirley about his leave or liberty from base duties. He was working the 2400 midnight to 0900 shift, which left little time for long trips around the Island of Oahu. He wrote:

"Dear Shirley. Remember how we kicked about not having enough liberties at Great Lakes? Well, here it is all almost the opposite. I could go out on Liberty to Honolulu or Waikiki every day if I wanted to because not enough goes on to fill the daily quota in our department. But my shift would not allow me to get much rest. Then, too, liberty is only from 10:30 AM until 5:30 PM each day. We can do as much here as on base except look at women."

"In our front yard, we have a beer garden, a bandstand for the Navy band or orchestra that plays every day, and a swimming pool. About 500 feet or less from the barracks is a theater that has three shows daily, and it's free about every other day. On the main floor of the barracks are a restaurant, a canteen, a tailor shop, a library, a large lounge and reading room, and a recreation room with pinball machines, bowling alleys, and pool tables. Why go out? I am going out in a few days to see the town and the famous Waikiki beach.... All my love and kisses, your sailor, CM."

Sounds more like a resort with light duty, but when the ships return from battle, it is 'all-hands-on-deck' to make repairs.

"Clyde, you ready to hit the beach? The bus to Waikiki Beach and the Royal Hawaiian Hotel is almost here," Harold said with anticipation. "Can't wait to put my feet in the cool surf."

"Just gotta grab my hat. Let's go!" Clyde replied with a big smile.

The old gray Navy bus rumbled up to the Pearl Harbor Naval Base bus stop, and the boys boarded. Black smoke belched out of the exhaust as the bus pulled onto the highway. They passed the landmarks of Hickam Army Air Base, the pink Tripler Army Hospital, Kalihi, Honolulu Airport, the Maritime Piers, and the Punchbowl Crater as they rumbled into Waikiki.

"Look at that beach! All those guys are swimming and lying on the warm sand. And I don't see any women, just GIs," Harold said with a sad look of remorse.

"Hey! There's the Royal Hawaiian. Wow. It sure is a pink color. Can't miss that place. I'm ready for a cool one," Clyde replied.

The two sailors got off the bus and headed directly to the hotel's United Service Organizations (USO) canteen. They paused a moment to listen to the US Navy Band playing at the pavilion on the lawn. In the USO canteen, they found most of the missing women and free coffee and doughnuts with snacks. They settled in to listen to the music and maybe find a friend or dance with one of the hostesses.

"Well, it's not the Aragon Ballroom in Chicago, but it's a lot better than our pool tables and pinball machines." Clyde said while keeping time with music by tapping on the table.

After relaxing at the canteen, the guys headed for the beach. There were only two hotels on Waikiki Beach in the 1940s, and they headed for Moana, a hotel built in 1901 on the east side of the Royal Hawaiian. Clyde rented a pair of swim trunks for a quarter and changed into them.

The cool surf felt great in the hot afternoon sun. The afternoon clouds were gathering and if they were lucky, it might rain a little and cool down the air temperature. In Hawaii, it rains a little every day.

"Boy, I haven't had a real swim in the ocean in my life. Not too many places to swim in Akron, Ohio, besides the Ohio River." Harold commented. "It feels so different. Like you can almost float if it wasn't for the waves...Look out, here comes a big one!"

Just then, Clyde got dunked in the wave and tumbled on the beach. Laughing, he said, "Now I know why those guys use those paddle boards. So, they can stay on top of the wave instead of under it! Let's get out a little deeper and try to stay on top of the waves!"

Laying on the hot sand felt good after the swim, but after a while, a cool drink was needed. Music wafted from the Moana Beach Patio cantina. It sounded strange, and they got up to investigate. "Clyde, what kind of music is that? Sounds Hawaiian, but what are those baby guitars? Not a banjo or guitar, too small." Harold laughed.

"I think they call them Ukuleles. They're playing 'Hawaiian' Country music." Clyde guessed. "I have seen the hula dancers and fire-dancing men in the movies and postcards." They paused to listen to the mellow sounds of the Island Singers for a few minutes.

They changed back into their white uniforms and made their way back to the USO canteen. Now, the beach was filled with all of the GIs that had the same idea of enjoying the day off in the water. "Harold, we better get a move on. It's 1630 hours, and the bus will be here in ten minutes if you don't want to be put on report for being AWOL?" Clyde said when he realized how late it was.

"Yeah, I'll grab my hat. It's been a swell time out here on the beach. Let's go!" Harold said as he took the last swig of his drink and of they ran to the bus stop. [16]

As they passed the turn-off for the Pali Highway, Clyde said, "Next time we have leave, let's try to see the windward side of the island. Guys say the trip over the Pali Highway is really pretty." Clyde was dreaming out loud. "You drive down the side of the mountain pass and see the whole island from there."

"Here's the base gate. Just in time. Better head down for Chow before heading back to the barracks." Harold suggested.

"I hope I have enough energy to write Shirley tonight. But that swim made me hungry. Let's get going!" Clyde replied.

---

[16] The US Navy took over the Royal Hawaiian Hotel and the beachfront of Waikiki in 1942, which was the largest and best-known hotel in Hawaii at that time and operated it for the rest and relaxation (R&R) of the submariners in port during their refits and repairs and operational training. As a Sub Base sailor, Clyde would utilize the beach on Waikiki as often as possible. It was the place he always talked about the most.

Thirteen - Faces of War

9 August 1943, Pearl Harbor "Hey! What's goin' on in this sorry sub-shop?" Sid called out to Clyde.

"Why, you dirty old salty sea dog! When did you make port? How's the new 'Lady Lexi' doing?"

Sid Soncek was a Torpedo-man Second Class (TM2/c) serving on board the USS Lexington.[17] The new aircraft carrier, CV-16, was named after its predecessor, the CV-2, which was sunk at the battle of Coral Sea in May 1942. The CV-16 arrived at Pearl Harbor on 9 August 1943. "We docked last night. She's still afloat and not too much damage from the last cruise in the Sea of Japan. I'm doin' as well as can be expected after a few months at sea."

"How long are you going to be in port?" Clyde hoped to have some company on his next liberty time.

"Well, not too long, a few weeks at most. Have to reload and refit by the end of October when we put it out to sea again. Scuttlebutt has it we're heading for the Gilbert and

---

[17] As strange as it sounds, a Torpedo Man serving on an aircraft carrier ship was common. A large complement of bombers carried torpedoes to sink enemy shipping. The same Mark 14 torpedo used in the submarines, with all its same faults, was adapted to aircraft use and launched from the air toward their targets. The same torpedoes were used in many other types of surface ships, like PT109 (Patrol boat Torpedo) skippered by LT. John F. Kennedy, who would become President in 1960.

Marshall Islands. I don't know when we'll make a berth in Pearl again. We have just a few hours left until we start loading fresh torpedoes. Got to make it to the base exchange for a few items. Just came by to say hello." Sid said with a tired look on his face.

Clyde smiled and replied, "Glad you did. I'll be working the swing shift with very few days off. There was no liberty for a while with all the subs and ships preparing for sea. We're still retrofitting the RADAR systems. We haven't got any of the redesigned electronics yet, so we're still retooling by hand to supply the fleet."

"Good. Those new systems are really hot." Said Sid.

"With a hundred boats left to rework, we'll be doing it for a while," Clyde said, wiping his brow from the afternoon heat.

"I'll try to catch up with you before we get underway. Say 'Hi' to Shirley for me. June's been writing fairly often, but her letters arrive fairly sporadically at sea. Good luck! Got to shove off now." Sid waved goodbye.

"Will do. Keep your feet warm and your powder dry." Clyde waved back.

9 December 1943. The proud and glorious "Lady Lexi" slinked slowly into the harbor at midday. Nicknamed the Blue Ghost, she was blackened from the fires onboard and listed slightly to the starboard side. Her fantail section was ten feet lower than her bow. A major Japanese air counter-attack began while the US Naval forces engaged in an attack off Kwajalein Island in the Marshall Islands. At 2322 hours, parachute flares from Japanese planes silhouetted the carrier, and ten minutes later, she was hit by a torpedo on the starboard side, knocking out her steering gear. Nine men were killed. The ship was reported sunk during the battle by Japan's Tokyo Rose. However, the crew made emergency repairs to the steering and flooded compartments, and after the battle, she made way for Pearl Harbor.

Clyde's duty shift was over when he noticed the USS Lexington docked nearby. An aircraft carrier was always a sight of great expectations. Her massive size invoked awe and amazement; when it docked, it was a good day for all. The tug boat slowly moved her massive hull into the berth, with her steel plates ripped and bent out of position from the torpedo. A crowd of sailors surrounded the blackened hull of the gallant fighting lady. Clyde joined the crowd to find out the story of the great battle and to find his friend Sid Soncek. The crew was released for shore leave almost twelve hours after she docked. Clyde was back on his usual shift that night.

"Hey Clyde! You in the shop tonight?" Sid yelled into the Sub Base Machine Shop as he opened the door.

"He's back in the office," one of the machinists replied.

"Hey, you old 'Landlubber,' what's going on?" Sid said as he walked into the office.

"Sid! Are you alright?" Clyde got out of his chair and offered him a big handshake. "We heard through the grapevine that the Lexington had sunk! I was so surprised when I saw it steam into port yesterday. You alright? Any wounds?"

"I'm okay. A little tired. It was HELL, though. With planes landing and taking off, it was crazy. It was just crazy when that torpedo hit our stern. Fortunately, only one torpedo hit its mark, or I'd be swimming in the Pacific Ocean. I was on the hanger deck fitting torpedoes on the bombers when the whole ship shuddered and pitched up and down. I fell on the deck and got up as the smoke began bellowing out of our starboard side. Eventually, we recalled all our planes because the smoke was so bad that they couldn't see the flight deck and land. And no friendly land bases close enough to arrive safely."

Clyde was awestruck by Sid's story. "Thank God it was not worse."

"We lost a couple of fighters in the beginning, but most returned safely. Over 2500 men were on board." Sid shook his head in agreement. "Hey, any news from the home front? Has Shirley said anything about June? The mail is really bad now. Only the Navy top brass know we are still afloat."

"No word about June in my latest letters from Shirl." Clyde nodded.

"When you write Shirley, tell her you saw me, and for her to tell June? June will never get my mail for weeks, and the Navy thinks it's a good idea to keep telling the Japanese that this ship is in Davy Jones' Locker," Sid asked.

"Sure. I'll write her today like always. That would send a good message to June. What's the orders for now?" he wondered.

"We think the plan is to patch up a few temporary fixes and repair the steering. It's been pretty much manual so far. There is no actual steering control from the bridge. Have to communicate all rudder and speed commands by intercom or radio. About a week or less here in Pearl and then head stateside for major repairs. It's a good thing that the propulsion screws weren't damaged. That's why we made Pearl in five days." Sid sighed. "Duty stations are twelve on and twelve off. That's the only reason I'm standing here. My shift was up, and I needed to stretch my legs."

"I'll tell Charlie Gerst you stopped by. Maybe if you get a little leave time, the three of us could run over to Waikiki for a little time together?" Clyde suggested.

"The rumor has it that as soon as we get some of these patches fixed, we'll head to Bremerton, Washington, to fix the rest of the major battle scars. That should take two to three weeks. Maybe I'll have time to see June in Washington, if I'm lucky." Sid smiled at the thought of seeing his bride again. "And when you write Shirley that you saw me and have her pass the news on to June. Mail from the States is really bad now. Mail-call is almost a monthly activity. I'll get sixteen or twenty letters at a time. She says that's the way it is in Antioch, too."

"The Fly-boys got the week off, but us deckhands have to stay close to the dock. I'll let you know if I get some leave time. Better run. Got to be back by 0600," Sid said as he stood and walked toward the door.

"Glad you stopped by. I'll let the gals know you're doing fine." Clyde shook Sid's hand and patted him on the back as they walked to the front door.

Two weeks later, the Lexington was headed for Puget Sound, Washington, for major repairs.

All types of warships entered and departed Pearl Harbor daily. But it was always a notable sight to see when one of the gallant ladies, large aircraft carriers or battleships arrived or departed Pearl, like the USS Lexington.

In early March 1944 the USS Franklin (CV-13) arrived from Newport News, Virginia, on her maiden voyage, sporting her fresh paint, shiny new airplanes, and a fresh new crew of two thousand plus sailors. The best that the 1944 US Navy had to offer. By mid-March, the Franklin was refueled and ready to join the Task Forces in the South Pacific arriving in Pearl Harbor 6 June 1944.

From the Submarine Repair Shop, nothing passed without notice. "Hey Clyde, look at the new carrier. Looks pretty new," commented one of the repair shop sailors. "Come and take a look!"

"Wow, she's a beaut! I heard that a carrier was due in soon. I think they call her 'Big Ben' Franklin. We'll have to swing by when the shift is over and give her an inspection," Clyde commented.

Almost fifteen weeks later the Franklin arrived in Pearl a second time. The Franklin was damaged in the battle of Leyte and returned to the mainland for repairs in September 1944. She was returning to war after her repairs at Bremerton, Washington.

Again, after refueling, she departed Pearl on 3 March 1945 to continue the fight with Japan. On 19 March, fifty miles east of Japan, a horrific battle ensued. She had two direct bombs dropped on the flight deck that penetrated the hanger deck where the ship's complement of planes, ammunition, and bombs were stored.

The aft section was immediately engulfed in flames, exploding ammunition and fuel-loaded planes, creating an inferno that could have easily taken the Franklin to the bottom of the Pacific. After six hours, the flames were extinguished, and the devastation became obvious. The enormous quantities of water poured aboard to fight the fires further caused the ship to have a 15-degree list to starboard, and her stability was seriously impaired such that her survival was in jeopardy. Gaping holes where the aft flight deck had been, fifty-nine planes were destroyed, and over a thousand sailors were killed or wounded. This was the second largest loss of life on a single ship, behind the USS Arizona. (disputed official numbers claim it could be higher than the Arizona).

Three weeks later, the Franklin was back in Pearl Harbor for temporary repairs so the ship could return to New York and the east coast shipyards. The ship was a black hulk of twisted steel, not easily navigable in the shipyard, even with tugboats assisting. The ship entered the docks too fast and crashed into the dock abutments with loud scraping and smashing noises as dockyard workers ran for safety. Just adding insult to injury.

"What the hell was that noise? Are the Japanese bombing us again?" The repair shop workers ran outside to see the decimated warship in the next dock.

"Clyde, get over here. The Sub-Base Commanding Officer (CO) wants all-hands-on-deck to help with the repairs of the Franklin. Clyde, contact your buddies in the other machine shops and see where we can lend a hand. She has to be underway in a few days, and the Pearl Harbor CO needs the dock space for the other ships coming in for repairs. Let me know what you need." The Chief ordered.

The USS Franklin departed at the end of March and arrived in New York on 28 April 1945. She would never return to the Pacific war with Japan.

As a Submarine Repair Shop worker, Clyde and the other machinists boarded almost every sub that arrived at Pearl. They would assist the crews with repairs or installations, like the SJ Radar.

The USS Wahoo (SS-238) was a regular at the sub base, arriving every six weeks from patrol for supplies and fuel. The day Clyde arrived in Pearl in February 1943, the Wahoo arrived and departed three days later. She had made a reputation as a straight shooter, having sunk nearly 20 Japanese ships (Top-ten shooter in the sub-service). Wahoo arrived on 29 August for regular supplies, sporting the victory symbol of the broom mounted upright on her periscope masthead signifying another good 'sweep of the oceans.' Everyone in the shop was proud that she was one of the Pearl Harbor 'regulars.' She departed in early September 1943 for the Sea of Japan. She never returned. She sunk in the Sea of Japan in October, six weeks later, on her way back to Pearl.

By the end of 1944, Japanese targets were dwindling, and some submarines were reassigned to perform rescue and reconnaissance support for large Naval Operations Task Forces. The USS Finback (SS-230), a Pearl Harbor-based submarine, was on its Tenth Patrol providing 'lifeguard duty' for downed American flyers. On the night of 2 September 1944, five Naval aviators were rescued by the Finback in the Pacific Ocean southeast of Japan and north of

Iwo Jima Island. One of the young aviators was twenty-year-old Lieutenant (LTJG) George H. W. Bush, who would become the 41st President of the USA. LTJG Bush remained on the Finback for thirty days, assisting with lookout duties until the sub ended its patrol and arrived at Pearl with its cargo of aviators. After its Twelfth Patrol, the Finback was in Pearl when the Japanese surrendered in August 1945.

Many more gallant sub-crews came and went, and a few, like the Wahoo, were lost. The Tang, Trigger, Sculpin, Seawolf, and forty-two submarines never made port again. But you can feel the relief with the remainder of the sub-crews that did arrive in Pearl with their stories of battle and secret missions and rescued pilots. The Tautog, Silverside, Flasher, Kingfish, Barb, and two hundred others survived to tell the tales of victory. By 1945, with the fixed/replaced Mark 14 torpedoes and SJ Radar, the submarine service had reduced the Japanese ship traffic by more than eighty percent, strangling Japan's military presence throughout the Pacific. The US Armed Forces knocked on Japan's backdoor - Iwo Jima and Okinawa.

Fourteen - VE Day

8 May 1945. With the Victory in Europe (VE) now in hand, May 8, 1945, was designated VE Day and a holiday. The world celebrated, except for the Pacific forces still fighting against Japan. Clyde wrote on May 10, 1945, that VE Day had come and gone, and the only difference was that they would work longer hours with no extra liberty. May 16, he wrote: *"Over here, you would never know that there had been a VE Day. I guess the stores and everything in town closed down, and all the churches offered prayers, etc. But as to us here on base, it was just another workday. That was about all everyone talked about in the chow lines or wherever a group got together, but other than that, it was the same dull day."*

However, reflecting on the Great Depression, which had preceded WWII, Clyde wondered what would be in store for their life next: *"I sure hope it is all over soon, but at times I shudder to think of what will happen when everything is peaceful. I hope there won't be depression or very hard times right away, but I can hardly see how it can be otherwise. I would like to be able to save enough to buy our own home and get settled before it gets too tough. We won't need a very big place, but I would rather have my place, or rather our place than have to pay rent all the time and worry if we can meet the next payment."*

Since Clyde went off to work in 1938 in Akron, Ohio, he has been sending money to his mother in Parkersburg each payday. The Navy paycheck was still small, but he was still sending money home to Mom, and now Shirley too. Shirley was saving it for household items or the wedding. Shirley was buying US Savings (War) Bonds with her money. Clyde said he had about $40 left over each month. Life in the Depression had taught him to watch every penny and save for the future. A long-distance call from Honolulu to Chicago would cost $15 for five minutes (almost two weeks' pay)[18] if you could get through at all. Then, with the time zone differences, the coin-operated phones, and the operators placing the calls, reaching the party you were calling was almost impossible. Remember, answering machines were still 30-40 years in the future.

With the Naval Censors reading every letter, it was hard to describe places and things without giving away the location of his duty station or assignment. Conversations and pictures were limited to only personal stateside activities and general comments. But by July 1945, Clyde had not yet been around the whole island of Oahu. One weekend, he and a bunkmate hopped on a Navy bus traveling around the island to the various bases and installations. There were lots of sugarcane and pineapple fields, and military installations, all off-limits or boring and repetitive.

"We did go around the island, but I'll know better next time. The bus was not a sightseeing bus; therefore, it did not stop at any of the points of interest to give you a

---

[18]Minimum Federal Hourly Wage in 1944 was $0.30/hour.

chance to take pictures. Could not take one from the bus either because it was a beat-up, rickety old trap that bounced around over the rough roads as badly as a 'Model T'. I'll try to hitchhike the next Saturday that I have leave and take pictures of the sights I see."

As in all times of war, the lower-classes and weaker people are taken advantage of, whether it is financial, property, possessions, or sexual. Clyde writes about the terrible insults that women received from the soldiers and sailors on leave in Hawaii. Clyde had suggested that maybe Shirley could come to Honolulu to be together, and she could get a civil service job because there were lots of openings. But he reconsidered when he wrote about the way women were treated. He did not want his "girl" to go through those degrading insults.

"When they [women] step out on the street alone or with another woman, there is always someone making a dirty remark out loud and stating how they would like to spend the night with them. It makes no difference who she is or how old she is; if she has some kind of shape or is not too ugly, there is always someone to make a pass at her…. No thanks, I think too much of you…to live among strangers and always be insulted."

Clyde tells of the 'city life' in Honolulu. *"Housing is so scarce that people rent [one-car] garages, put in a cot, and maybe a cook stove and a table, and they have room for a whole family. Gasoline is about the only thing that is actually rationed, but there is such a shortage of meats and vegetables that it is pitiful… The cost of living is so high that a dress that costs only $5 in the States, costs $15 here."*

In July 1945, Shirley was living in Antioch with her parents and helping with her father, who had heart health problems. She was working for her Uncle Ted Poulos in his candy shop. Clyde commented about her working at the candy shop and how he would have lots of nieces and nephews when they got married, hopefully sooner than later. Shirley sent a photo of the nieces and nephews in front of the candy shop in 1945.

"The war in Europe had ended, and our workload had evolved to the point that the command could start granting 30-day 'stateside' leave periods to a few 'long timers' each month. I was granted leave to commence in August 1945, and in mid-July, was sent by troopship to San Francisco and then by ferry to the Mare Island Submarine Base, Vallejo, California." Clyde wrote.

Fifteen - Coming Home

30 July 1945, Monday. Antioch Illinois. Phone rings. Theodora, Shirley's younger sister, ran to answer the phone. "Hello!"

"Hello, can I speak to Shirley, please? This is Clyde McLain." There was a pause.

"I'll see if I can find her." Thea, hoping it was her friend, put the phone down and yelled, "Shirl, it's for you."

"Who is it?" Shirley asked. Thea replied. "I don't know. Some guy. Think he said Clyde something."

Shirley ran to the phone. "Hello!"

"Hi Shirley, this is Clyde. I got a thirty-day furlough from Pearl. I'm in San Francisco. I'm boarding the train tomorrow for Chicago. I'm hoping you still want to get married!"

"Oh, oh, ah, yes. Of course, I do. Are you really in California? Why didn't you let me know you were coming?" She tried to recover from the shock of the news, thinking maybe this was some kind of a joke.

"Can't talk long. The call is costing one dollar a minute, and I'm almost out of change. Will send a telegram with the train schedule," said Clyde.

"Oh, Clyde, I can't believe you're almost here! Are you sure?" she replied.

"Yes darling, we've been writing about this for two years. I'm ready. I love you, Shirley!"

The Operator interrupted, "Please deposit another dollar or hang up."

"Gotta run. See you soon." Clyde hung up the phone.

"Mom! Mom! Where are you?" Shirley screamed.

"Stop yelling; I can hear you fine. What's the matter?" Sophie said as she wiped her hands on her flowered apron.

"Clyde just called from California. He's on his way here so we can get married!" Shirley exclaimed. "What am I going to do? He'll be here by Friday!"

"Well, now, that is a big surprise! Are you sure you want to marry a sailor you haven't seen in two years?" Sophie shook her head in disbelief.

"Clyde and I have been discussing this for a long time. He has even been sending money to help pay for the wedding from his Navy paycheck every month. We have a lot of work to do if we're going to have a wedding," Shirley exclaimed.

"Yes, daughter, we do have a lot of work to do in a short time. I can talk to the church ladies and see if we can get enough ration coupons to make a wedding cake. We'll need to talk to the Methodist minister to reserve a date, and where can we hold the reception? You know we have a large family and need a big room for the whole gang. Okay, I'll help get the word out that we're going to have a wedding! Oh, and what about a wedding dress?" Sophie exhaled as she walked back into the kitchen to finish cleaning up from dinner.

"Hello Bets? Clyde just called. He's in California and will be here Friday. He wants to get married! Can you believe it? Bets, I want you to be my bridesmaid. Thea will be the Maid of Honor. Oh, and, and? I don't know. It's coming up next week. Bye, talk later," Shirley said in a hurry.

That night, Sophie and Shirley made a list of all the wedding details and who they would invite. The Hennings family was quite large. With the five daughters and their families, aunts and uncles, and school friends, the total number of guests could easily be between thirty and forty people.

Shirley asked her mother, "It's been a long time since he has seen me. He may change his mind after he sees me again. Better to wait to buy anything until Clyde is here and he sees me and has reaffirmed his marriage proposal."

"But, daughter, it will take a week to put this together. Are you sure? That means we won't be able to have a wedding before Wednesday, August 8, at the earliest," Mom replied.

"I want him and me to be sure about this wedding," Shirley said.

2 August. Thursday. Doorbell rings. The Western Union Messenger delivers the telegram: *"Ogden UT 803 PM Aug 1 Miss Shirley Hennings Antioch Il STOP Arrive Furlough Challenger C&NW Station 9:20 AM Friday STOP Love Clyde McLain STOP."* Shirley read the words and thought about how she would pick up this sailor from the station.

"Dad! Can you take me to the Chicago train station early tomorrow morning?" She showed CE Hennings the telegram.

Scratching his head, CE replied, "Well, I should be finished with my newspaper deliveries by 7 AM, and we can drive in after that. Should make it by 9 AM with no problems."

"Thanks, Dad. That'll be swell!" Shirley smiled in delight.

3 August. Friday. As the 1940 Chevrolet sedan pulled up to the Chicago and North Western train station on Madison Street, it was a beehive of activity. People are coming and going in all directions. After parking the car, Shirley and CE hurried into the station to find the train and track number. It was about 9 AM. An ocean of uniformed sailors and soldiers moving in every direction greeted them at the stairs. The Furlough Challenger Train (1944-1945) was a special troop train for GIs only returning from the war. The train would be easy to locate, but how to find Clyde in the sea of sailors in blue uniforms with white hats was a bigger problem.

The Challenger Train was only a couple of minutes late pulling into the station. Considering the three-day and two-night journey from San Francisco, it was "on time." The GIs start disembarking on the track platform, walking toward the station gate door. It was pandemonium as almost 1,200 GIs get off the train and are looking for their bags and family or friends.

Shirley and her dad got as close as possible to the gate doors and spied every white hat that approached.

Occasionally, she would call out "Clyde?" to someone who might look familiar. Ten minutes passed, then twenty, then thirty minutes. The stream of GIs never slowed. Shirley was in a panic and was searching frantically. The California train cars were at the end of the twenty-car train, and they were the last GIs to get their bags and walk a quarter mile into the station. Finally, Shirley screamed, "Clyde, over here!"

She could hardly believe her eyes. It really was that skinny West Virginia sailor that she remembered from two and a half years ago. No words now, just hugs and kisses and more hugs. At one point, Clyde paused to shake the hand of CE Hennings. Clyde had carried his duffel bag, set it on the pavement, and started to speak, "Well, I finally made it. Only fourteen days from Pearl Harbor to Chicago." He caught his breath and continued, "You sure look great. You're prettier than I remembered! Let's get outta here." Clyde picked up his bag with one hand and slung it over his shoulder, then grabbed Shirley's hand with his free hand, and they walked toward the station doors.

As CE piloted the Chevy toward Antioch, the conversation was a thousand questions and answers punctuated with a kiss or hug in between. The whole family came out of the car as they arrived. Everyone wanted to hug Clyde and introduce themselves. Ten or twelve nephews and nieces giggled when Clyde and Shirley would kiss. Sophie hugged her newest son-in-law and welcomed him to the family.

The whole family stayed late into the day, asking questions about the Navy, the war in the Pacific, and what it was like to see the carnage of the Japanese attack on Pearl Harbor. As the party broke up, Clyde took up temporary residence with Uncle Ted Poulos, who lived in a small house on Spafford Street with his sons Peter and Tom. Ted's wife, Phyllis, had died in 1935 after the boys were born. It was like having a bed at the YMCA while the family was planning the wedding.

Later in the day, Shirley visited the Minister of the local Methodist church and set the wedding date of Wednesday, August 8. Now, the Hennings family attended the Methodist church, but Sophia's family was Greek Orthodox. The little town of Antioch only had three churches: a Methodist, a Roman Catholic, and an Episcopal. The Greeks have hated the Catholics since the thirteenth-century Sack of Constantinople. So, Sophia could not go to the Catholic church, so they went to the Methodist church. However, the Methodists did not allow alcohol in the building.

"Where are we going to have the reception dinner after the wedding?" Shirley asked her mom. "There aren't any restaurants big enough to hold the whole family, and it would cost too much. What are we going to do?"

"Let's call Friar John at Saint Ignatius Episcopal church and see if we can rent their Fellowship Hall for the evening," Sophie suggested, "And we can have our wine served and toast our usual Ouzo. Opa! Opa!" Sophie said as she did a slow twirl in the kitchen.

"Good idea! Now, what about food for the reception? With the war rations, we can't buy enough food to serve everyone. Maybe we could get the families to bring a potluck-style meal to share with everyone?" Shirley thought out loud. "That leaves only the Wedding cake and Wedding dress!"

"Let's ask Uncle Ted if he could make the cake for us, if we give him our ration coupons to buy the flour and sugar. You know he's the best candy maker in Illinois," Shirley suggested.

"Yes! Ted is the perfect one to do the cake. I'll call him later and see what he thinks," Sophie said, "And Ted can never refuse my special requests; he is a great family man, and you take care of the boys and work at his shop. I know he would be honored to do that for you."

"Okay, that leaves the biggest problem, the wedding dress. Any ideas?" Shirley wondered.

4 August. Saturday. The afternoon was getting hotter, and Clyde was helping Ted in his candy shop, where it was cool, just to keep busy and leave the women alone. Clyde was banished from their company because there was 'women's work' to be done before the wedding. Clyde enjoyed the conversations and light-duty chores. Sweeping, cleaning the display cases, and maybe serving up a soda for a customer once in a while.

"How does it feel to be away from the war and relax a little?" Ted asked.

"It's very strange. No loud noises, no one yelling at you to hurry up, no battered ships docking and wounded sailors being carried off. No oil or grease on my hands from the machine shop tools. A guy could get used to this quiet life!" Clyde smiled.

"Ted, where did you learn the art of candy making? These chocolates are beautiful. No wonder Shirley enjoys helping you out at the shop now and then!" Clyde inquired.

"Well, after I came to this country from Greece in 1914, I worked in the ore smelter in McGill, Nevada. Money was always in short supply, so I looked for other ways to bring in some cash. For a couple of years, from '22 to '23, on the weekends, I was a pro wrestler on the Reno and Las Vegas wrestling circuit. It paid well but was too hard on my body. But I met a Greek in Reno who came from Logan, Utah. He said his family had a candy company there. I quit the smelter and got a job at the Politz Logan Candy company, where I learned about this candy business. In '24, I was out of work again. Came to Chicago in '25 and met Shirley's sister, Phyllis. We started a restaurant here in town. Then Phyllis died in a car accident in '35 when the boys were young, and it was too hard to raise kids and run the restaurant at the same time. So, I started this here, Sweet Shop, where I can work around the boy's schedule. That's when Shirl started helping out raising them boys." Ted smiled, "That's a long answer to a short question."

"So, Ted, you've been really great letting me bunk with you and the boys. Thank you so much. But I have a favor I'd like to ask you if it's okay with you?"

"Sure, anything for a sailor who's going to be my brother-in-law in a few days," he replied.

"I have a problem; I don't know anyone here but you and the Hennings clan. Would you stand up with me as my Best Man? I'd be much obliged if you could." Clyde looked directly at Ted and smiled.

"Why, of course. I'd be honored to stand up for you anytime. I suppose I'll have to dust off my old suit in the closet and polish these old shoes. When is the wedding?" Ted laughed and smiled.

"The gals say the wedding is on Wednesday evening. You'd better be there to keep me from getting shaky knees or passing out. Shirley would skin us both. Ha, ha." Clyde laughed.

"Say Clyde, why don't you go check on them boys and see how they're gettin' along with their chores? I can handle the store, and you need a little time to unwind and relax after that long journey from Hawaii. Thanks for the help." Ted smiled.

"Sure, sounds like a good idea. Maybe I can throw the ball around in the back with the boys later." Clyde waved goodbye to Ted as the shop doorbell tinkled softly.

5 *August. Sunday.* The Sunday sun was warm when Shirley and the family left for the Methodist church. Ted and Clyde joined the family at the church. Clyde was introduced to the congregation in uniform, and they were anxious for news of the war in the Pacific. After the service, the family conversations reconvened at the Hennings' house.

"Clyde. What's happening at the Poulos house today?" Shirley asked.

"I think Ted and your other brothers-in-law are getting together to plan a dinner party. Maybe a 'bachelor party' for yours truly," Clyde said with a grin and a little apprehension. "What are you doing today?" he asked.

"We will be going to both churches to talk with the women about decorations and preparations for the dinner. Did you know that with the war, it is almost impossible to get fresh flowers? We'll cut some roses for the tables and different flowers for the bouquet. There's not much to do for the dinner decorations. I think we've invited about fifty or sixty people. Glad we were able to get in the Episcopal Church," Shirley explained. "Tomorrow, we may be going to the city to look for the wedding dress and bridesmaids' dresses."

"Great, I'm sure you'll be a beautiful bride! Just three more days! Can't wait to see you again!" Clyde replied with excitement. "I think my host is leaving with his boys, so I'll see you later. Love you!" Clyde said as he kissed Shirley and gave her a big hug.

"Well, I'll be around Ted's Sweet Shop or hanging out with his boys. Sure do miss you. I haven't seen you since Friday." Clyde remembered, "Oh yeah, I forgot. On Tuesday, I have to pick up my sister Freda at ten o'clock in Chicago. I think Einar Petersen is driving me to the station. I guess it's a busy day for you folks. I'll call you later. Love you, sweetheart."

6 *August. Monday.* Shirley was frustrated with the wedding dress problem. At breakfast, she let out a sigh, "I can't find any dress in Antioch that I like. Can we go into Chicago to *Marshall Field's* department store? They have a bridal shop. I know it's going to be expensive, but there's no time to hand-make a dress and get it fitted by Wednesday. What do you think, Mom?"

With Sophie and Thea sitting at the table with their coffee, Sophie agreed, "Yes, that may be the best solution. Why don't you call Betty Hanké, and the four of us can catch the train into the city."

"Great idea. I have saved over fifty dollars, which goes a long way if they have any dresses I like and can fit into without alterations. Maybe we can catch the 10 AM train from here," Shirley said with excitement. "Yes, it could work. I'm going to call Bets right now."

"Hi, Bets. Are you doing anything today? Want to go to *Marshall Fields* and look for my wedding dress? We thought we could catch the 10 AM train to the city." Shirley quickly took a breath. "What do you think?"

"The office is closed today for factory maintenance at *Pickard China*. It'll be a swell time. Sure! I can get ready and meet you at the train station. Sounds like fun." Betty thought. "And maybe lunch there too! See ya later."

The three Hennings' women got ready, and Sophie drove them to the Antioch train station, where they met Betty Hanké.

"How are the wedding plans coming along? Is this the last thing to do?" Betty asked.

Shirley recited details to Betty. "And Uncle Ted will be Clyde's Best Man."

The morning air was cool as they boarded the train, but the weather reports were afternoon thunderstorms. Sophie said, "We should make the Chicago Loop in about forty-five minutes. Walk to State Street and the *Marshall Field* Building."

Traffic was normal on Monday morning. Horns honking, pedestrians hustling across the intersections, people talking and yelling, just another noisy Chicago day. Finally, they reach State and Randolph streets and enter the gigantic twelve-story building. Take the elevator to the Sixth floor and *The Dress Room*. The faster they walked, the faster the conversation went until they reached the Dress Room clerk.

Shirley asked. "Miss, where are your wedding dresses?"

"Right this way, please." The clerk led the four women to the Bridal Shop. She asked the usual questions, "Size, color, style, price range?"

"Here you are, Miss. I'm sure you'll find something to your liking here. When you are ready to try one on, just wave, I can assist you with the fitting. I'll be just over there."

"Too much, too little, don't like it, … How about this one? What do you think? Should I try it on?" Shirley said as she waved the gang to come over to her.

The gang closed in around her and looked at her choice. They agreed that it might work. Betty called the clerk to assist Shirley with trying on the new dress. Someone said, "Oh, look at the lace veil and the long train in the back." Shirley followed the clerk to the fitting room. In about ten minutes, the preview appearance began. Shirley walked carefully out of the fitting room toward her family. Turned slowly and paused. "What do you think? Seems to be a pretty good fit."

Everyone stepped closer to touch the fabric and look at the embroidery and lace. Smiling and commenting to each other, "It looks great. How's the fit?"

"It's a little long. It needs to be hemmed a couple of inches. The train is detachable. Sleeves will be all right," Shirley commented.

"If you want this dress, we can hem it in an hour or two while you continue shopping. Just up on the seventh floor is the Alterations department. What do you think?" asked the clerk.

"Well, Bets and Thea need the dresses too. Maybe they could find something while we can get mine altered. Okay," Shirley suggested. "Mom, what are you wearing?"

"Oh, don't worry, Shirl, I have my eye on a navy-blue chiffon gown over there. I'll try it on when you gals are finished." Replied Sophie.

The bride's maids began to look over the selection while the clerk took Shirley's measurements for alterations. Shirley changed back into her street clothes and helped the gals find their special dress. Bet's found an aquamarine blue dress, and Thea chose a light-yellow dress. The clerk took their measurements and sent all the dresses to the Alterations department. Shirley gave Sophie the fifty dollars she had saved. The bill for three dresses, three pairs of shoes, and miscellaneous items was less than two hundred dollars. About six months pay for those gals.

Relieved that the dress problem was under control, Sophie said, "Anyone hungry? How about lunch in the *Walnut Room* on the Seventh floor? I'm buying!"

The four ladies moved up the escalator to the dining room for lunch. The large open room with skylights letting in the afternoon sun was a perfect place to discuss all the little details of the approaching wedding. It was hard to remember that a war was still going on, and rationing was everywhere. After VE Day, people felt less stressed and very hopeful that Japan would soon surrender and join the ranks of defeated Germans.

With all their packages in hand, Sophie decided to pay for a cab to the train station instead of walking. As they rode the train back to Antioch, Shirley said, "I bet Clyde thinks I've left the state or something."

The next couple of days were a beehive of activity: calling guests, meeting with the church women about the wedding details, planning the dinner, and finding ration cards for food. Shirley was planning the honeymoon trip to Janesville, Wisconsin. Clyde had received good news that his older sister, Freda, would be arriving the Tuesday morning the day before the wedding from Washington, DC. Freda's rank was Seaman First Class in the regular US Navy.[19]

7 August. Tuesday. Clyde and Einar headed to the Chicago Union Station to meet sister Freda McLain. They entered the sea of uniformed GIs, embarking and disembarking their trains. Freda arrived on the *B&O's #9 Chicago Express* train at Chicago Union Station. Track 17. Eventually, Clyde spots Freda, "Hi Freda, over here!" Pushes his way through the crowd to her. Hugs and kisses and smiles. "Where's your bag? When do you leave DC?"

Freda was dressed in her best US Navy blue uniform and hat. She was excited to see her younger brother in civilian clothes. Einar catches up to the two and introduces himself. "I'm Einar Petersen, Clyde's new

---

[19] Freda McLain had enlisted in the regular US Navy in 1942. Her rank was Seaman First Class. She worked in the Pentagon in Washington, DC, and if you asked what she did, she would reply, "If I tell you, we both will go to prison." After she passed in 1998, we discovered that she worked in translation of Japanese military radio messages, which were then sent back to the US Pacific armed forces. The Japanese never knew that the USA had broken their military code with the help of our Japanese-American citizens.

brother-in-law, almost. I'm married to Shirley's sister, Leona. Welcome to Chicago!"

"My bag is still in the train car. The porter has not brought it out yet. It's been a long night. I left DC at 10 a.m. and had to sleep on those hard coach seats. Nice to be here. Say, do you guys want to grab some breakfast? The dining car was full, and ran out of food. I need a quick snack. How far is Antioch?" asked Freda.

"About 35 miles, but with the traffic about an hour or so. There's a snack kiosk with the Sun-Times newspapers over there. You can grab a Baby Ruth candy bar or peanuts before we head to the car." Einar pointed to the newsstand inside the terminal.

The porter dropped off her bag from the luggage cart, and Freda indicated she had two strong men to carry it. On the way to the parking lot, they grabbed a snack and a bottle of Coke Cola for the trip.

The Hennings family eagerly greeted their new family member with hugs and handshakes. Freda looks very commanding in her US Navy uniform and hat with proper military regalia. Photos taken with everyone and kids running around with great enthusiasm and loud voices. Freda got settled in at the Hennings house. Later in the afternoon, she visited with Clyde and Ted before returning to Shirley's house.

After the Hennings family introductions, Freda spent the day at Ted's house talking with Clyde and Ted and the boys. Clyde had not seen Freda since he was shipped to Pearl in February 1943. The topic of discussion was the recent news from Parkersburg: Sister Ellen was getting married.

Mother Viola and Ellen were traveling to New York City for a wedding with Charles Brown, an Atlantic sailor in the US Navy. Ted and Clyde dropped Freda off at Shirley's place for the evening with the gals.

"Come on, Clyde, time for dinner and a few bottles of beer with the boys," Nels Petersen said. Nels is married to another one of Shirley's sisters, Elaine. "We've got to get to the restaurant on Main Street. The guys thought we needed a little party since all the womenfolk are at Sophie's house having their party." They loaded up the car and headed to town.

Meanwhile, the gals were having fun without all the guys. Betty, Thea, Shirley, June, Kay, Leona, Elaine, Freda, and half a dozen others were having fun and a few glasses of wine before dinner. The evening continued until Sophie went to bed, and some said they had to work in the morning. "See you tomorrow," they shouted as the group broke up and returned to their homes for the night.

Sixteen - Atomic Weddings

8 August. Wednesday. The Hennings' house was ablaze of activity early Wednesday morning. The final checklist was reviewed, and items were checked off the list. Freda left early to have breakfast with Clyde and catch up on the latest news from Parkersburg, West Virginia.

"Who's picking up the cake from Ted's shop? At what time?" Shirley asked. "What about the food for the dinner?"

"The Methodist women are picking up the cake and food and bringing it to the Episcopal Church," Sophie said, "Einar will bring the wine when he's off work today. I think all you girls need to do is relax and work on your hair and get your dresses ready." She paused. "Leona is getting the flowers for the Methodist Church later today. She'll have your white gladioli bouquet and the orchids, roses, and asters for Thea's and Betty's bouquets. So, there's not too much to do until six o'clock."

"Mom, I sure love these Bride's Maid dresses; they're so pretty. I'm so glad we could find everything in one store. I just could not seem to find anything in Antioch, not without a month's notice." Shirley smiled. "Clyde and the guys have it so easy. Clyde only has to wear his Navy uniform, and Ted just wears his Sunday suit."

"Shirley, have you seen the flower-girls' dresses? Sigge Petersen is wearing a peach-colored dress, and Betsy Frazier wears a blue dress. They'll be so cute with their baskets of rose petals." Sophie laughed.

8 August, Evening. The church ladies decorated everything, and flowers were arranged throughout the church. The music played, and the candles shimmered on the church altar. Reverend Sitler was up front talking with Clyde and Ted when the music paused, and then the '*Here Comes the Bride*' music began. The audience stood to greet the bride after the bridesmaids and flower girls had spread their petals on the carpet. Shirley was adorned in a white eyelet embroidery dress, over which fell the long veil and train carrying her bouquet of white gladioli. She was escorted by her father, CE Hennings.

"Dearly Beloved, we are gathered together tonight…." Reverend Sitler began. As Clyde joined hands with Shirley and stepped up toward the altar, the service began with the usual solemnity and excitement of the moment. Ending with the ceremonial lifting of the veil and kissing the bride.

"Friends and family, I want to introduce you to Mr. and Mrs. Clyde C. McLain," announced the Reverend as everyone stood and applauded. A few cheers were heard. As the new Bride and Groom walked down the aisle together, it was barely 8:30.

After a few obligatory photographs of the wedding party, everyone departed to the Episcopal Church for the long-awaited dinner. The Bride and Groom greeted their friends and family with hugs and kisses as they arrived at the dining hall.

The wedding party was happy, and their conversations were lively. A few toasts for the new couple and some usual speeches and storytelling continued late into the night. The four-tier wedding cake was sliced and served in the traditional way. Finally, the bride and groom said goodbye for the evening. As usual, some left because of work; some stayed late and partied into the evening.

Clyde borrowed a car from one of the family members and drove to Janesville, Wisconsin. Shirley's family donated several gallons of rationed gasoline for the trip. Friends had tied a few old tin cans on the back bumper and wrote "Just Married" on the windows with lipstick. Clyde drove the sixty-five miles to the Monterey Hotel, built in 1929, on the corner of High and West Milwaukee Streets in Janesville, Wisconsin. With its Art-Deco styling, the Monterey was a landmark in the region.

9 August, Thursday. "Hey Shirl, listen to this, *'Atomic bomb dropped on Hiroshima!'* the newspaper headline read. Would you believe that? The first ever atomic bomb! It says a B-29 bomber named Enola Gay dropped the atomic bomb, Little Boy, on the Japanese city. Gee, that is going to be a great help in the Pacific War." Clyde read. The news was three days old, which was fast for the war reports in 1945, which could take weeks to reach the home front. The newlyweds toured the Dells of Wisconsin and returned three days later.

Mid-August. Clyde wanted to visit Parkersburg with his new bride so that Shirley could meet his family. Taking the Washington Express out of Chicago's Union Station, they changed trains and arrived in the early morning. Sister Freda said goodbye on the train and returned to Washington, DC.

The old McLain family house on Myrtle Street in Parkersburg had long needed a fresh coat of whitewash paint. The two-story house overlooked the Ohio River and looked about the same as Clyde remembered it. He only visited it once, in January 1943, since he had lived in Akron and enlisted in the Navy. The house was two miles from the Ohio River on the rise and was regularly assaulted by the river when it flooded in the Springtime.[20] As the taxi from the train station pulled up in front of the house, the family came out of the front door and stood on the porch waving to their guests.

"Hi Mom, glad to see you again. This is Shirley, your new daughter-in-law," Clyde said, turning to sister Ellen McLain, now Mrs. Brown. "Congratulations on your wedding last week, August 9."

"Thanks, and congratulations to you folks, too," Charles Brown said. "Ellen and I had fun exploring New York City last week... The Statue of Liberty, Times Square, Central Park. Didn't have enough money to take in a Broadway show, but hey, at least I'm on dry land and not onboard the ship for a couple of weeks. Have to be back onboard next week when we head out to the Atlantic with more cargo. I can sleep a lot better now, knowing that the Jerry's in Europe have surrendered. Their subs were causing all kinds of hell for us Merchant-Marine ships."

---

[20] In 1937, the water came to the back steps and flooded two feet of the basement. The 1937 Ohio River flood caused the river to crest at twenty feet above its banks and caused great damage along the river banks in Ohio, Illinois, and West Virginia. The Army Corps of Engineers soon created dams and ponds up and down the Ohio River to relieve the high-water dangers.

"I have to leave on September 1 for Mare Island, California, so I can catch the next ride back to Pearl. Not looking forward to that. Did you hear about the atomic bomb last week in Hiroshima?" Clyde commented.

"I hope this Atomic bomb business slows down those Japanese." Charles replied.

"Did you hear we dropped a second bomb on Nagasaki on your wedding day, Charlie? Between the Iwo Jima and Okinawa Island battles, our boys are getting kicked pretty hard as they get closer to Tokyo. Hoping the Pacific War will be over soon," Clyde said.

"Yeah, me too!" Charles shook his head in affirmation.

"What'd you say, we all go inside, get out of this heat, find a cold drink, and talk inside?" Clyde suggested. Everyone agreed that was a good idea. Mother Viola McLain led her guests into the house.

Clyde told the whole story to Ellen and Mom about the work in Pearl and returning home to marry Shirley. The family time was light-hearted and cordial as the new family members tried to bond and swap old stories of childhood experiences in Parkersburg. Charles Brown had to leave the next day for his ship in the New York City harbor. Ellen and Viola drove Clyde and Shirley to the train station two days later for their return to Chicago.

Seventeen - Family Life

Last week of August. Clyde and Shirley are back in the Hennings' house in Antioch. Sophie was cleaning up the breakfast dishes while Clyde was explaining his plans. "Saturday, I have to get on the train back to Mare Island on September First or Second. It takes three days, and I need to check in by the Fifth. The train leaves at about 10 AM. Need to get tickets and reservations. The same C&NW Furlough Challenger will be heading westbound to California. The US Navy doesn't like stragglers coming in just whenever they please."

Time was short, full of surprises, love, and enjoyment, especially after being in Pearl Harbor for thirty-one months without more than a day off now and then. Shirley and her dad, CE, drove Clyde back to the Chicago C&NW train station. Lots of hugs, tears, and kisses made the separation less painful, but Clyde had accomplished what he came to do: marry the girl of his dreams, who had been waiting for over two years to be together again. The train left the station on time and headed southwest to St. Louis, Omaha, Ogden, and Sacramento before stopping in Martinez, California. Buses were waiting to take sailors to the Mare Island Naval base.

The Western Union Telegram read: *"Arrived on time September 5. Letter to follow, I love you Clyde % CE*

Hennings, Antioch ILL" and a second telegram on September 8, *"Happy [one month] Anniversary. Got your letter and pictures today. What a happy anniversary gift. Hope you are well. Love you, Clyde."*

10 September. Clyde writes, *"There is good news: The war is over!! But I must stay here until they decide which sailors will be sent home, which will go to their home recounting office (like Akron, Ohio), and who goes back to the war as the police action begins in Japan. So, I wait and will write you and sometimes a call. The Navy will decide in the next few weeks or months who goes where."*

10 October. Clyde writes, *"I have to go straight to Akron to be discharged from the Navy. The train will pass through Chicago for several hours. Maybe you can visit me there for a little while? I have to take the Southern Pacific train to the Chicago Union Station and transfer to the train going to Akron. About an eight-hour layover. Will send a WU Telegram when underway. Love you. Soon we'll be together again."*

During the Second World War, Chicago's Union Station alone handled over three hundred trains and 100,000 travelers a day, most of whom were GIs. There were several smaller stations for rail traffic, but Union Station was the most heavily used to move troops.

Shirley spent the night in Chicago with her grandmother. In the morning, she caught the bus to Union Station. Arriving at 10 AM, she looked over the sea of uniforms. With so many GIs coming home, the crowds were twice as large as in September. She slowly made her way to the track for the Southern Pacific eastbound arrival. She had about thirty minutes before arrival. The hustle and bustle of the travelers forced her to find a seat in the waiting room until the train arrived. It was almost like waiting for a celebrity to appear on stage. Her excitement and anticipation continued to mount as the minutes slowly dragged on. Finally, the steam engine's bell was ringing as the train slowly came to a stop! PUUUSHHH! went the sound of the air brakes on the train. Then, the passengers began the slow process of disembarking. Finally, there he was, just as handsome as ever in his US Navy blue uniform.

"Clyde! Clyde! Over here!" she said as she pushed forward into the sea of travelers.

"Shirley! So glad to see you. I missed you so much!" Clyde said as he embraced her and kissed her. They quickly moved to the trackside and into the waiting room. More hugs and kisses. They exhaled, and both tried to speak at the same time. Laughing at each other, they began again.

"How long have you been waiting for the train?" Clyde asked.

"Not long, only a half hour or so," Shirley replied. "Let's go outside and find a coffee shop and get out of this noise so we can talk." And they headed for the Canal Street doors.

Clyde explained the Navy's Discharge Plan for returning GIs. They discussed some ideas for post-war life: where to live, job opportunities, family matters, and gossip about the other Gang of Antioch GIs still in the armed forces. They walked around the Chicago streets holding hands and hugging now and then. They made their way back to the station about four o'clock. The time went so quickly, but they knew the new life was almost here and planned the phone calls and letters he would write. At the trackside, the "All aboard" call came out loud and clear. Finally, the last hug and kiss. Waving to Clyde as he steps aboard the train. "See you soon. Love you!" Shirley said with tears in her eyes.

17 October. Clyde received his Discharge Papers from the USN Separation Center in Toledo, Ohio. Clyde returned to Antioch the next day as an unemployed civilian with a month's pay in his pocket. He began his new life as a married man looking for a job and a place to settle.

Epilogue

October 1945. "I returned to Antioch, and after a short vacation, Shirley and I traveled to Akron, Ohio, and set up housekeeping. I then returned to my former place of employment, The Goodyear Tire & Rubber Co, which, by law, had to give me employment. It was also my first 'cold' winter after having spent three winters in Hawaii."

Betty Hanké had two brothers in the Army, Allen and Leslie. She lived with her mother, Nellie, in a house where she grew up. Allen was drafted early in the war. He was with the 3rd Armored (tank) Division in Europe. He was killed in action and is buried there. Leslie went in near the end of the war and was injured in a land mine which took off part of his foot. After two years in the Veterans Hospital, he came home to a "fairly" normal life in Antioch. Betty married Lenard Fischer on January 17, 1948. Len could not serve in the service due to heart issues caused by rheumatic fever as a child. They lived in the same house until Len passed in 2014 after celebrating sixty-six years of marriage. Betty lived near her daughter in Illinois until her passing in 2018.

Clyde's sister Freda met Gail Wharton in 1935 before the war began. Gail served in France and Germany as a Platoon Sergeant. They were married several years after the war and lived in Parkersburg with Clyde's mother. Freda and

Gail never had children. She was very proud of her service in the Navy as a Japanese codebreaker in Washington D.C.

Clyde's younger sister Ellen married Charles Brown, also a sailor, on August 9, 1945. Charles served as a Chief Gunner's Mate onboard a Merchant Marine ship that supported the assault on Anzio, Italy, and later the D-Day assault on Normandy, France. His ship was based in New York, where they were married during the August 1945 furlough. They lived in Vienna, West Virginia, near Parkersburg all their lives. They had one daughter named Gail.

"In the spring of 1946, we packed up our car and a small trailer and headed for Antioch, ILL. Shirley was a few months pregnant, and her Mom and Dad convinced us to stay in Antioch until after the baby Michael was born. I worked for her father as a part-time Newspaper Truck Driver and with the father of one of Shirley's schoolmates, who installed gasoline pumps, garage equipment, etc. I found permanent employment at The Hough Co. in Libertyville, ILL, in their Machine Shop as a Machinist. They made street sweepers, bulldozer blades, etc."

"One summer day, one of Shirley's school classmates, Leona (Hostetter),and her Husband Charlie Doerr, their one-year-old son, and we were on a picnic, and they revealed that a friend in California had offered Charlie a job as a plumber in Azusa, California and that they were making plans to move there."

"We told them of our thoughts and plans to go to California, and they invited us to go along with them and share moving expenses, etc. We bought a stake body truck to hold all our furniture, and finally, in November 1947, the

caravan of 2 cars, a two-wheel open trailer behind our car, and the large Stake body truck covered with tarps got underway. We decided the big truck had to be reloaded for proper balance and stability, so Charlie and I set everything out on the ground and loaded up again. This time, it improved the ride and steering, and we made the long trip to Colton, California, without any serious problems."

"We arrived in Colton the day before Thanksgiving and moved into a house their friend had arranged for them to rent. The Friday after Thanksgiving, I went to the employment office, and they referred me to the US Department of Agriculture's Experimental Laboratory in Riverside, where I was immediately hired as a combination Mechanic, Machinist, Carpenter, and Jack-of-all-trades. My immediate Supervisor was a Civil Engineer who had worked on the team that had perfected the rocket launchers used so successfully during the war. "

"When the Doerr's moved to Azusa in mid-1948, we moved to another house in Colton and eventually purchased a house in Riverside. In the spring of 1948, to supplement my income, I worked part-time at a service station, dispensing gasoline, washing customer's car windows, doing lube jobs, and other miscellaneous jobs around the gas station. At about the same time, the US Naval Reserve was opening a branch office in nearby San Bernardino and recruiting new members who would receive pay for attending a meeting once a week. With the thought of more income, I volunteered and once again was involved with a branch of the Navy. Their recruiting campaign was successful enough to cause them to build a fairly large training center in San Bernardino."

"Following the outbreak of the Korean War in June 1950, I was recalled to Active Duty in September 1950. Shirley's parents and two nieces came to California to pick up their house trailer that had been parked in our backyard and took Shirley and the children back to Antioch to stay with them. Shirley needed help to take care of Mike and Baby Chris until I returned in 1953."

From Clyde C. McLain's Memoirs

End Notes

In October 2006, Clyde, 86, came back to Pearl Harbor, Hawaii. He visited the USS Arizona Memorial and walked the decks of the USS Missouri as if he were a young 23-year sailor again. He climbed the ladders up and down the decks with a renewed vigor that had been lost over the years. We located the old sub-base Evacuation Training Tower, which had been used in WWII, and the buildings near his sub-base repair shop. Tears came to his eyes as he reflected on those years of love, fear, and hopes for a better future. Shirley died four days before their 61st Wedding Anniversary on August 4, 2006. Clyde joined his bride again on June 7, 2008.

Clyde was always a patriotic man and taught the family how to respect all people, and especially the country for which he gave his best years of service.

Clyde visited his old friends Betty and Lenard Fischer in June 2007 for the last time in Antioch, Illinois, almost 65 years after they met. Betty was the last to pass in 2018.

These people were all part of the Greatest Generation, and our lives are richer for their sacrifices. We pray that those left behind will always honor their memories by living up to the ideals that they lived by: Love of family, Faith in God, Fellowship with neighbors, Loyalty to friends, Honor and Respect to all, Responsibility for your actions, Courage and Perseverance in the face of difficulties, and Patriotism to this United States of America.

Photos 1

L to R: Clyde arriving in Antioch, Wedding photo, Honeymoon Janesville,

Photos 2

L to R: Troop ship, Aragon Ballroom Chicago, Royal Hawaiian Hotel, Mark 14 torpedo and control, Freda (McLain) Wharton, Freda's Pentagon Japanese Translation group, USS Wahoo "Clean Sweep", USS Arizona Memorial

Photos 3

L to R: Clyde & Charlie Gerst, Charlie Hostetter & Sid Soncek, Clyde & Sid Soncek, Clyde & Charlie Hostetter at Royal Hawaiian Hotel, Salvage of USS Utah, USS Franklin (3) on fire, underway, Kamikaze damage.

Photos 4

L to R: Submarine Base Sign Today. Map of Pearl Harbor, Sub Base aerial in1940s, Arrow at Sub Rescue Training Tower.

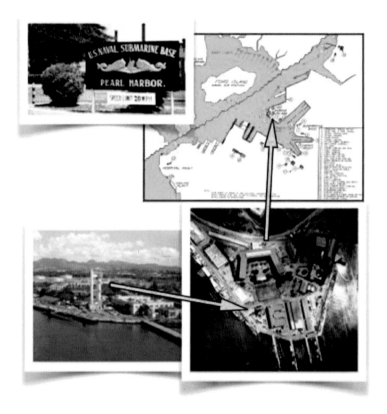

About the Author

Mike McLain lives in Idaho. He grew up in the shadow of US Navy Bases in California and Hawaii. He worked in the early computer and printer service industry from 1966 to 2002, with experience in farming, ranching, and motorcycling. Mike has traveled throughout North America, Europe, and Asia. Since 2002, he has focused on charitable causes in Guatemala, Mexico, Nicaragua, and Cuba.